Katie Cox vs.
the Boy Band

Also by Marianne Levy

Katie Cox Goes Viral

KATIE COX vs. THE BOY BAND

Marianne Levy

sourcebooks jabberwocky

Published by Sourcebooks Jabberwocky, an imprint of Sourcebooks, Inc.
P.O. Box 4410, Naperville, Illinois 60567-4410
(630) 961-3900
Fax: (630) 961-2168
sourcebooks.com

Originally published as *Face the Music* in 2017 in the United Kingdom by Macmillan Children's
Books, an imprint of Pan Macmillan.

Library of Congress Cataloging-in-Publication Data

Names: Levy, Marianne, author.
Title: Katie Cox vs. the boy band / Marianne Levy.
Other titles: Katie Cox versus the boy band
Description: Naperville, Illinois : Sourcebooks Jabberwocky, [2018] |
    Summary: "Katie Cox became an overnight pop sensation, but can she face
    the music of the public spotlight?"-- Provided by publisher.
Identifiers: LCCN 2017052011 | (pbk. : alk. paper)
Subjects: | CYAC: Singers--Fiction. | Fame--Fiction. | Friendship--Fiction. |
    Bands (Music)--Fiction. | Fathers and daughters--Fiction.
Classification: LCC PZ7.1.L4897 Kd 2018 | DDC [Fic]--dc23 LC record available at
https://lccn.loc.gov/2017052011

Source of Production: Berryville Graphics, Berryville, Virginia, USA
Date of Production: April 2018
Run Number: 5012071

Printed and bound in United States of America.
BVG 10 9 8 7 6 5 4 3 2 1

So there I was, standing in the wings, ready to do my first major concert. I mean, seriously major, with tons of people watching and goodness knows how many more online.

Even though I'd practiced and practiced, I was shaking so badly I could barely hold the guitar. My hands were dripping sweat, and there was a good chance that when I opened my mouth, I'd barf all over the stage.

It was no use telling myself that everyone gets nervous. Because this was no ordinary concert.

I was about to sing live to twelve and a half thousand people.

And each and every one of them wanted to kill me.

Chapter One

LET'S REWIND.

So basically, I recorded a song in my bedroom. A song called "Just Me." I've always written songs, ever since I can remember, and sat in my bedroom and sung them. Like using up all the hot water and leaving my homework on the bus, writing songs is just something that I do. And this song wasn't especially different from the others.

Except that my friend Jaz put it on YouTube. And it went sort of viral.

Okay, a lot viral.

It started with everyone at school and then went sort of crazy. Like, being-played-on-Top-40-level crazy. Lacey said that her aunt went to Thailand, and "Just Me" was coming out of the speakers there. It's kind of upsetting that my song gets to go to Thailand when I've never managed to get any farther than Plymouth.

Anyway, I ended up getting signed to a record label

called Top Music, which I still can't really believe, because this is me we're talking about. Katie Cox: pizza lover, boy band hater, and possessor of the world's wonkiest bangs. Being signed to Top Music meant all kinds of things.

It meant I had my song go to number two on the charts. It meant that I was supposed to be writing music for a concert and an album. And it meant that I was with the same record label as the annoying boy band Karamel.

This last point wasn't particularly significant, except that, in a moment of extreme foolishness, I'd promised my class-mate Savannah that I would get her tickets to go see them, and she would not let me forget it. Seriously, the girl was obsessed.

"Katie, you know those Karamel tickets…?" and "You did promise me, Katie." and "It's, like, completely fine and everything, but they are touring right now, and you made me a promise, and if you don't keep it, I will tell the entire Internet about the time at my birthday party when you fell into my cake. I have pictures, Katie."

We were at school, sitting in the bushes behind the back of the science classrooms. You'd think that a number-two-selling pop star would, maybe, have more glamorous places to be.

In fact, a month had passed, and I hadn't seen any money from my mega hit, and even if it did ever turn up, Mom had assured me there was no way I was allowed to spend it on starting a new life in Hollywood. And for all my pleading, I wasn't entirely sure I wanted to live alone in a mansion made of gold. At least not until after the end-of-semester dance.

"All right, *fine*," I said.

"Really?" Savannah's face was shining like I'd opened up her head and stuck a tea light in her mouth. "Babes, you are rocking my world. Backstage passes, yes, yes?"

You would also think that being a number-two-selling pop star would elevate me into a position at least slightly above Savannah, even if she was the richest and prettiest girl in my class.

Oh well.

I started texting the head of Top Music. "I'm asking, okay?" I held it up to show her.

"Ew!" said Savannah, who had seen far too many American high school movies. "You cannot seriously expect me to go on my own."

"I seriously can."

Savannah went gray, which is pretty hard to do when you're slathered in spray tan. "Katie. You are asking me to meet my future boyfriend while looking—" She paused, her mouth making funny little shapes as she tried to bend her lips around the word *unpopular*.

Now, there is a big difference between looking unpopular

and being unpopular, and unlike Savannah, I have experienced both. So even though, really, I think Savannah would probably benefit from a dose of unpopularity, I softened enough to say, "All right. I'll ask for two tickets."

Sofie and Paige sat upright, and Savannah's head swiveled from one to the other. In the space of ten seconds, she'd gone from wounded possum to queen cobra.

"Pleeeease can I come?" said Sofie. "I will give you anything you want, Savannah."

"I'll give you double," said Paige. "My fake Gucci purse even. Anything."

"But that's not fair!" cried Sofie. "I don't have a fake Gucci purse to give!"

I am not one to mess with a friendship as beautiful as the Sofie-Savannah-Paige triangle, although I have to say, I did consider it. But the fallout would have been too great, both for the world and its fake Gucci leatherwear.

"Three tickets," I said. "I will ask for three tickets."

"Thanks, Katie."

"Thank you!"

"Can you make it four?" Now this was a surprise.

Because the words had come from my best friend, Lacey.

Lacey, who had always agreed with me that boy bands are an insult to music. And that the worst and most insulting boy band of all is Karamel.

"Hahaha," I said. "You're funny, Lace." She wasn't laughing back.

"Yes or no?"

"Lacey, you cannot actually be suggesting that you want to spend an evening watching Karamel."

"It's either that or watch TV with Mom," said Lacey, who, to be fair, does have quite a scary mom.

"But—"

"I want to go," said Lacey. "It'll be fun."

"Four tickets," I said. And then I hit Send.

"Aren't you coming?" said Lacey.

"I am not," I said. "On account of Karamel being literally the worst boy band in the whole universe. Also, I have tons of other things to do. I am so busy right now."

"Whoa, have you *still* not written your song?" said Lacey. "What's the holdup?"

"There's no holdup. It's going great," I said quickly, and then looked hard at my phone until everyone started talking about something else.

This is the difficulty with having a song do well on the Internet. It starts out all exciting and awesome and everyone says "good job" and sends the link to their cousin in Australia and maybe you even get a record deal and end up on the front page of the *Harltree Gazette*.

And then, just as you're getting used to everything

being sort of awesome, it happens. Someone says, "So what's next?"

And once one person's said it, they all do. It's not enough that there's a song out there, a song you're really proud of, that everyone's been clicking on and singing at you in drugstores. Nope.

They want more.

Have you written the next one yet? When's it out?

We can't wait!

In fact, I had some potential next ones. More than some. Lots and lots. Hundreds, really, because I've been writing songs since I was little.

Only, somehow, even though I had notebook after notebook full of lyrics, most of them didn't seem quite right. For example, last night I found one I'd started a while back, about spaghetti hoops, and in my memory, it was really funny. But when I sat down and actually sang it, it was just this weird unfinished thing about spaghetti hoops. I mean, spaghetti hoops are nice and all, but I'm not sure they deserve their own song.

I still had plenty of decent ones to play Tony, though. And, as I said to myself, over and over and over again, it's only natural to have the jitters—absolutely nothing to worry about.

"Actually," I said, interrupting a conversation about

Karamel's latest album artwork, "I'm going into Top Music tomorrow to play them some stuff. And I'm sort of feeling a little anxious about it."

"I'm not surprised," said Lacey. "If I were you, I'd be really worried."

"Would you?" This seemed remarkably insensitive, coming from my bf. "Huh."

"Why isn't he replying?" said Savannah, who was more interested in my phone than my creative process. "Didn't you make it clear that this is important?"

"Savannah, I texted the head of one of the country's biggest music labels. I'm not sure that arranging your concert tickets is right up there on his list of priorities."

"So you *didn't* make it clear that it was important. Honestly, Katie, becoming a celebrity has made you so self-centered."

My phone flashed.

Everyone leaned in, Savannah's fingers doing this sort of grabby motion, like one of those claw machines you see at the arcade that always pick up the teddy bear and then drop it at the very last second, making you spend your entire allowance on a stuffed toy you don't even want when you actually needed the money for a hamburger and fries. "It's a yes," I said. "Next Thursday, four front-row VIP tickets will be waiting at the box office, plus wristbands for the backstage party afterward. All taken care of. Any problems just speak to security. Oh. Next Thursday is July the ninth. That's—"

I stopped talking because the screaming had gotten so loud and so high that no one would have heard me. It was like someone had stomped on a box of bats.

"Oh my God, I am going to meet Karamel!"

"They are so beautiful!"

"This is it. This is the best thing to ever happen to me."

"I am going to marry him. This is where it begins. Me and Kurt. Forever!"

"No, *I'm* going to marry him."

"No, I am."

The squeaks paused for the tiniest second, and I opened my mouth.

"Can we all just calm down a minute here and—"

Which is when Savannah said, "*What am I going to wear?*"

And after that, I could have said anything at all, to be honest, because no one would have heard me.

So I tried to meet Lacey's eye, with my *Wow, these three are being strange right now* face.

Only, she wasn't looking at me. She was looking at Paige and saying, "Do you think Kristian will talk to me? We could double-date…"

And I did wonder whether me and my best friend were ever so slightly growing apart.

Just a little.

"Katie, babes, are you okay? Because you are making the most ugly face right now."

"Thanks for letting me know, Savannah."

"No problem."

"Actually," I went on, "I am a little upset. Because July the ninth is—"

Only the bell was ringing, and Savannah and Paige and Sofie and Lacey were swinging off across the parking lot, chanting, *"We're going to see Karamel!"* at the top of their lungs.

I sighed and said, "July the ninth is my birthday."

But they were too far away to hear.

Spaghetti Hoops

They're orange
And they float in soups
They're pasta
And they're shaped like hoops

Something something spaghetti

Something something

~~Confetti~~

~~Yeti~~

No.

Argh!

Chapter Two

H ANG ON," SAID MY BIG sister Amanda, who had been scrolling through the latest celeb gossip on *Pop Trash*, but now put her phone down to focus on my stupidity. "You offered half your class free tickets and backstage passes to see the biggest boy band on the planet, and you're upset because they said yes?"

Mands has a very annoying way of seeing things sometimes.

"They should know better," I said. "Well, not Savannah's group. But Lacey should."

"Why?"

Honestly. "Because Lacey *hates* Karamel."

Amanda raised one of her eyebrows. "Does she? Or do you?"

And then she did the big-sister thing she does where she attempts to look really, really wise.

I couldn't even tell her to go back to her own room. Back in the spring, Mom and her new boyfriend Adrian had teamed up to buy the world's most useless house, and we'd all moved in together.

You wouldn't think that a house *could* be useless, since all it really needs to do is stand there without falling down. But our house wasn't even managing to do that. There were cracks in the walls, and the garage roof had collapsed, and when they finally got an inspector to come by he said that one side of the house had subsidence and urgently needed underpinning.

Which is a fancy way of saying that it might fall down.

So now the half of the house with the most cracks in it was strictly off-limits. Which meant that Amanda's room was out of bounds. Which meant that she'd had to move in with me.

I'd been trying to look on the bright side of things. It was much easier to borrow her stuff when it was sitting in the same closet as mine.

And…actually, that was pretty much the only positive thing. I mean, she's my sister and everything, but is it really necessary for her to fold her pants? Or make my bed? Or make me listen to every last track released by Friends of Noom or the Zits or whatever weird and unknown band she's currently into?

"We both hate Karamel," I told her. "Boy band? More like boy *bland*." I waited for some acknowledgment of what had been quite a smart thing to say, but Amanda's face wasn't moving, so I continued. "Lacey and I have always been extremely clear on that. They are the three most annoying boys on the face of the earth, and they have stupid hair. Their names all begin with a *K*. Even Kolin. I mean, come on. Kolin! And they can't sing."

"Kurt is a very accomplished singer and a terrific guitarist," said Mands. "How much Karamel have you actually heard?"

"I try not to listen to them!" Now I really was getting worked up.

"So you agree that you could be wrong?"

By this time, I was seriously considering permanently moving into Amanda's old room. Yeah, there was every chance it would collapse and kill me, but if I stayed in the presence of my older sister for very much longer, then I was going to kill her.

"I think I might go out for a while," I said.

"Don't you have a history essay to start?" said Ms. Annoying. "And a song to write?"

"Yeah, well," I said.

"And aren't you going in to see Top Music *tomorrow*?"

"Yes. And…"

"Katie, do you have anything to play them? Anything at all?"

"There's a song about spaghetti hoops," I said. "It's… it's not very good." I threw myself facedown onto my bed, which had a bowl of cornflake mush on the pillow, which I didn't notice until it had gone everywhere. "Uuuugh."

"Well, if you're going to leave food there…"

"I can't write, Mands. I forgot how to do it! I sit down, and I stare at the page, and nothing seems to come out, and I don't understand. And now I have cereal gunk in my nostrils."

She squatted beside me and handed me a T-shirt to clean up the mess. And actually, when I looked up and saw her expression of genuine concern, I felt a little shiver of fear.

"Katie, of course you know how to do it. You just need to start believing in yourself again."

"I do believe in myself! I know I can write songs. What I don't know is why I can't seem to write them *at the moment*."

"Ugh," said Amanda, which seemed to sum it up.

"I'm going out for some fresh air," I said.

♪ ♫ ♬

So out I went, off down the lane, doing my usual pause at the corner before the bus stop in case my fellow classmate and all-around weirdo Mad Jaz was there. Not that I was avoiding her or anything; it's just helpful to have some warning before you see Mad Jaz because of her being so mad.

Like, a few months ago, this young teaching assistant guy scolded her for wearing nonregulation tights. No one knows how she did it, but the next day when he came into school, all his hair had fallen out. Even his eyebrows.

Or how she's apparently been banned from every single branch of Lidl supermarkets. Not just in Harltree. Not even just in Essex. She's been banned from every branch in the *world*.

The bus stop appeared. And phew. She wasn't there. I continued on, down toward the main road, half thinking I should go back. That's the problem with walks. You have to have a plan before you set off, or they feel sort of pointless.

Then my phone started to go off. It was Dad.

I answered on the third ring.

"Dad! Hi!"

"How's my little superstar?"

"Really well, thanks."

"House still standing?"

"Of course it is," I said, because the only thing worse than living in a falling-down house was admitting it to Dad. When he and Mom had divorced we had to sell our old house, and somehow he'd managed to rent an apartment in America with his half of the cash, right on the beach, while we ended up in chaos. His place looked like the kind you'd go to on a vacation. No—correction. It looked like the kind of place Savannah would go to on a vacation. And Savannah gets her jeans from Harrods.

"Great! And how's your new career?"

"Um. Actually, Dad, I could use some advice on that. I've got this big meeting tomorrow with the record label, and I'm supposed to play them a bunch of new stuff. Only, I haven't written anything."

When I said it out loud, it sounded very, very bad.

"Easy! Just play them some of your old stuff and tell them it's new. They won't know the difference."

"But…I played lots of it at the concert in Adrian's shop."

"Like anyone remembers exactly what you played."

It wasn't the best solution, but it was a solution. "Okay, maybe I'll try that."

"How is Mr. Scuzzy Record Shop?"

"Adrian? He's really well, thanks. And the shop's so busy. You know Mands is working in there full time now, and she's doing this gig night once a week with new bands. It's been selling out." There was this pause, and I was clearly supposed to ask him about his new partner too. I lasted as long as I could, which was two seconds, and then I said it: "And how's Catriona?"

"Not so good," said Dad.

Which was a first. Ever since he'd gone stateside, Dad's life had been 100 percent fantastic.

"Er, how do you mean?" I said. "She's not sick, is she?" I knew as I said it that she probably wasn't. I mean, Catriona is a twenty-five-year-old vegan Pilates instructor. They don't get sick. They can't.

"She's found a new direction."

"What direction was she going in before?"

"Katie, Catriona and I have decided to uncouple."

Ah.

"Oh, Dad, I'm sorry," I said, which wasn't necessarily true, but he seemed glad I'd said it.

"Probably for the best," said Dad. "Because of the apartment."

"Still seeing dolphins from the kitchen window?" I asked.

"Yes. No." He cleared his throat. This was turning out to be the strangest Dad conversation ever. "The dolphins haven't gone anywhere. But I have."

"But why?"

"I needed a change, okay? A man can have too many dolphins."

"So where are you living now?"

"Well," said Dad. "I thought I would head over to see you guys for a little while. While I'm between places."

"Seriously?" I thought my heart might tear out of my

chest and explode. "That would be terrific! When were you thinking? Next month? Or is that too soon? Sorry, that's probably too soon, isn't it?"

"I can't wait until next month to see my best girl. How about…next week?"

"Next week? Wow. Yes. *Yes!*"

"Hold on—" There was a pause and some tapping. "Confirmed. Sorry, I was just buying the plane ticket."

"*Great!* Will you bring your guitar?"

"Sure thing-a-ling."

"I can't wait," I said, because I couldn't.

"Got to go, Katie. But—can I ask a quick favor?"

"Anything."

"Could you tell your mother for me?"

"Sure," I said.

"Love you, K."

"Love you too, Dad. I'm so glad you're coming home."

Well, after that, I was practically dancing. I know this because three cars on the main road slowed down to honk at me.

So I swung back up toward our street, noticing how the air smelled better and the sky was a little more blue.

And maybe I should have spent a little more time looking at what was going on straight ahead rather than sniffing the breeze and tilting my head at the clouds.

Because I neglected to do my usual around-the-corner check and therefore didn't notice Mad Jaz heading my way.

She was wearing this top that was half-red netting and half-slashed black shiny stuff, along with a truly epic level of liquid eyeliner.

I did consider pretending that I hadn't seen her and to keep on walking, but I decided against it. Jaz and I are sort of friends these days, although it's a slightly uneasy friendship, at least from my side of things, since it's based partly on liking Jaz but also partly on fear.

Also, Jaz had seen me and was calling, "Katie!"

"Hi, Jaz," I said.

"How's the song writing?" said Jaz.

"Oh, you know," I mumbled. Then, to change the subject to something I actually wanted to talk about, I said, "My dad's coming home. From America! Maybe he'll be back for my birthday? He said next week, and my birthday is on Thursday…"

"I thought your dad was that guy you live with."

"Adrian? Ugh, no! Adrian is Mom's boyfriend. No. My dad's this cool musician who lives in California. And he's coming back next week."

"Okay," said Jaz.

"So I can't stay and chat," I said. "I have to go home and tell Mom."

"Why are *you* telling her?"

"He asked me if I would."

"So he dumped it on you? Nice of him."

"It was actually," I said. "Dad wanted me to know first. We have this really special relationship. And anyway, Mom will be fine with it. She has Adrian now."

Jaz fell into step beside me. "Has he always been in America?"

"No," I said, speeding up in the hope that maybe she'd drop back and go away. She didn't. "He moved there a few months ago after the divorce. He got this cool place by the ocean. You can watch dolphins from the kitchen window. Well, you could before. He just moved out." Then, as I thought about it, I said, "Maybe there's a chance that he's back for good. How cool would that be?"

"Depends," said Jaz. "Was it one of those good divorces where everyone stays friends?"

I really wanted to say yes. But I couldn't. It had pretty much been the opposite of that. "Not especially," I said.

"And your mom thought he was safely in America. Only now he's back in just a few days, and he wasn't even brave enough to tell her himself, so he got you to do it," said Jaz.

"That is a very twisted way of looking at things," I told her. Although I have to say, the sky had gone back to its normal color, and I could definitely detect a little bit of car exhaust on the breeze.

We'd reached my front door. "Good luck," said Jaz.

"What for?"

Jaz smiled. "Katie, you are about to tell your mom that your dad, who she hates, is coming home next week, and that he was too cowardly to tell her himself."

"Honestly, Jaz. It's no big deal. See you Monday, okay?"

And then I was back in the hall, with its familiar smell of dampness and a strange sort of soupiness that we'd recently traced to a particular patch of carpet.

I couldn't go upstairs, not with you-know-who in my bedroom. So I went into the kitchen instead.

"Katie, love!"

"Oh, hi, Mom."

"Are you all right? Did something happen?"

I was going to tell her. I really was. It's just, I don't know, maybe Mad Jaz had spooked me during our conversation.

"No," I said. "Nothing happened."

"In that case, why haven't you done your chores?"

"Because," I said, trying to keep the wobble out of my voice, "I have a very important meeting with my record label tomorrow, and I am *trying* to write a song."

Chapter Three

I THINK IT'S FAIR TO SAY that as far as my music career is concerned, Mom is not a fan.

This is for a number of reasons. Some of them are fair enough. Others are completely nuts.

- And I do appreciate that this is a big one—Tony, the head of my record label, had sort of tried to destroy my entire life to get revenge on Mom's new boyfriend, Adrian. So yes, all right, I can see why she might have a few trust issues when it comes to Top Music. I kind of have them too, even though ever since my single made the charts, they have been very nice, sending me chocolates and cards and more flowers than we have vases to put them in (i.e., two).

- Mom figures that it will stop me from putting any effort into my schoolwork. I pointed out to her that I never put much effort into my schoolwork anyway. This did not seem to help.
- Dad is a musician. This means that I am not allowed to be a musician too. No, I don't understand this one, either.

After the whole single-going-viral-concert thing had happened, Tony had taken Mom and Adrian and Amanda and me out for dinner in London at this ultra-glam restaurant called the Ivy. Me and Mands had spent most of the meal celebrity spotting (we saw Amanda Holden, Stephen Fry, and someone who we are fairly sure was in *Game of Thrones*), while the adults had talked about contracts and percentages and things I wanted to be interested in, but somehow found I wasn't.

By the end, and after a couple of glasses of champagne, Mom had been smiling and had even let Tony kiss her on both cheeks, although once he'd gotten into the back of his fancy black car outside, she'd said, "I don't trust that man as far as I can throw him."

But it seemed that she had agreed to "see how things go," which, when I had quizzed Adrian later, meant she would let me record an album, as long as I didn't take even a single morning off from school, and that any money I made would be put into an account I couldn't get to until I was about seventy.

"And the second the music business makes you unhappy, then that's it, game over," Adrian had said.

"Of course," I'd said.

So on the morning of going in to see Top Music, I made sure to seem especially upbeat, singing in the shower and eating three of the four slightly stale croissants Adrian had found on sale at the store.

"I still don't know, Katie," said Mom, looking down at a sea of pastry crumbs. "I just think—"

"I *know* what you just think," I told her. "And I'm just saying, let me try it. If I don't like it, I'll stop."

We'd already had this conversation about seventeen times in the last week. I really couldn't see why we needed to be having it again now, when there was a train to catch and people waiting for me.

Which I told her. And she sighed. "It's going to change you, Katie."

"Er, I don't think so."

"Well, what if it changes the people around you? How are you going to feel when your friends start treating you differently? Some people are weak, Katie, and who knows what they'll do for a little attention, an envelope full of cash…"

"Like who? Lacey?"

"I don't want to see you hurt," said Mom. "That's all."

"I know," I said. "But I won't be. Adrian'll look after me. You trust *him*, don't you?"

I said this knowing full well that Mom would not be able to say that, no, she didn't trust her boyfriend. And then, just as I'd hoped, she gave me a kiss and headed to the hospital for her shift, leaving me to exchange a look with Adrian and swipe the final croissant.

"Katie, hello! And, Adrian! My friend! So great to see you both."

And then there we were in Top Music's great big glass meeting room—me, my guitar, and Adrian.

That was our side of the table. In the middle there was a plate of (what I knew from past experience would be really delicious) cookies. Then on the other side sat Tony Topper, the head of Top Music, with his rich-man stubble and bright white teeth and skin that would make an orange feel pale.

"So we're just finalizing the details for your first concert," said Tony.

"Er, okay. Um."

He leaned forward, and I wondered how he got his shirt so incredibly ironed. Maybe he just wore a brand-new one every morning. That's what I'd do.

"You seem a little worried."

"Well, yes. I've never done a big concert before. I mean, the only one I've done was in the shop, which is tiny and in Harltree and full of moldy old vinyl records." But then I remembered the shop's owner was sitting next to me. "But you know, completely supercool."

"It's okay, Katie," murmured Adrian.

"All I'm saying is that…I'm a little bit worried about it," I said. "Not, you know, super worried. Just averagely worried. The normal level of worried."

Tony showed me a mouthful of expensive teeth.

"No problem, Katie. We'll keep this first one pretty small, okay? More of a showcase than a concert. Intimate and low-key. Just have some industry people in, a select group of fans, a few friends, and that's it." He took a sip of coffee. "And of course, we'll put the word out that you're playing and then make sure no one can get tickets. That's always a good way to generate buzz for a new artist. Get you trending on social media."

I'm sorry, but there is literally nothing more cringey than when a grown-up says "trending on social media."

Tony may be a humongously successful music boss with all the world's money, but "trending on social media"? Er, I don't think so.

"And if it all goes well, we'll have you playing Wembley

Arena soon enough. So"—he nodded toward my guitar—"are you ready?"

Which is when I kind of got a little panicky and spent far too long tuning, during which Adrian ate two cookies and got crumbs all over the table.

"Okay," I said eventually when I couldn't put it off any longer. "So this is 'Cake Boyfriend,' which is kind of my favorite song from everything I have. I mean, it's maybe not single material. But I think it should definitely be on the album. Maybe."

And then I started to play.

Now, here's the thing. I wasn't at all feeling it when I started. But music's sort of like magic, isn't it? Not that I believe in magic, but if I did, I'd say that songs are spells, and as you're singing them, you're kind of pulling everyone around you into this glimmery bubble where nothing else matters. It's just you and the music.

The song finished, and I stopped and smiled, feeling a little giddy.

And Tony said, "That's fine, I guess. Anything else?" Then I played through "Song for a Broken Phone," only Tony said that most people get free upgrades on their cell phone contracts and are really glad when their phones break since it gives them an excuse to get a new one.

So I played "London Yeah," only Tony said that it

was too UK-focused, and I needed to think about foreign audiences, and so I sort of gave up and concentrated on eating the remaining cookies, which in fact weren't quite as nice as I remembered.

"Katie, forgive me if I'm wrong," said Tony, who did not look like a man who thought he was wrong or who thought he needed to be forgiven, "but didn't you play all these songs at the record-shop concert?"

I mumbled, "Maybe…"

"Do you have anything new? Anything at all?"

"I've got the beginning of a song about spaghetti hoops," I said.

The awkward pause that followed lasted for something like infinity.

"We'll send over some ideas," said Tony. "And it's great that you're coming to the Karamel gig. Kurt's a real fan of yours."

"Oh, I'm not actually—"

"You two should collaborate on something."

"Er."

"Great, I'll run it by him." He saw me eyeing what was left of the cookies. "Have one! They're here for you. And congratulations again, Katie. We're so excited."

"Me too."

"Just, try not to put too much pressure on yourself, okay? With the writing. It'll come."

"Okay," I said through a big mouthful of cookie.

"If you can," said Tony, "try to go for something incredibly universal, that'll really translate. Something that your fans can latch on to, like they did with 'Just Me.' Funny but serious. Introspective but upbeat. You know the kind of thing."

"Um, yes."

"We're certain you'll come up with it very soon."

"Um, yes."

"I'm sure you're feeling as confident about Katie as I am," said Adrian, giving my shoulders a squeeze. A couple of months ago this behavior would have qualified as unacceptable, but now, I must admit I was grateful for it.

Especially when I reached for another cookie, and Tony said, "About that."

"The cookie?"

"Yes. This is a little delicate, Katie. But you're going to be in the public eye a lot soon. And I'm sure you'll agree that it would be great for you to go into all of this really feeling…and looking…your best."

Was Tony calling me fat?

"So if you'd like a personal trainer or for us to get you on a meal plan, just let us know. Top Music is here to help."

He was!

"Thanks," I said. "I'll, um, keep that in mind." I pushed the plate away.

"I've got to get back to it now—conference call to the Glastonbury Festival people. Remember, I'm on the end of my phone, day and night, if you ever want to play anything for me."

"Okay."

"Don't let the pressure get to you," said Tony. "The last thing we want is for you to experience some kind of creative block."

I must have looked startled as he coughed.

"Crystal Skye had one after her first concert. We waited and waited, and eventually we locked her in a hotel room for a week."

"And then she wrote a new song?" said Adrian.

"No, she had a nervous breakdown!" said Tony, getting to his feet, which meant we had to do the same. "But *then* she wrote a song. So it worked!"

Chapter Four

JAZ IS ONE OF THOSE people who seems to take up a lot of room. I'm not saying she's big or anything. In fact, she's a lot thinner than me. It's just she has this really enormous aura that fills up all the space you put her in, whether it's my bedroom or our classroom or, as with right now, the top deck of the bus. I hope we don't ever get stuck in an elevator together. I'd probably suffocate.

"You've got a lot of Amy Winehouse stuff," said Jaz, scrolling through my iTunes, which was a little surprising because I hadn't given her my phone. The thing was far too precious to ever leave my hand, being new and nice and literally the only thing that had come out of all this fame stuff so far.

Also, I'm not hugely trusting of Jaz around phones because of how she managed to film me on hers, put the video online, and made me go viral, with the result that I almost lost my best friend, alienated the rest of my school, and almost broke up Mom and Adrian.

I reached out and took it back again. How she got it in the first place was beyond me. I made a mental note to keep it in a zippered compartment. Maybe two.

"Amy's music is amazing," I said, gazing out the window, and then turned back as the bus smacked into the branches of an overhanging tree. "She only did two albums, but every single track is just, you know..."

"How's your album going?" said Jaz.

I'd always thought it was best, with people like Jaz, not to ever show any sign of weakness because they'll just use it against you later. But recently I'd changed my opinion of her. Not that I'd decided she was the world's nicest person or anything, but she had been, well, sort of, kind of nice.

Which is why I felt like it would be okay to say, "Not as well as I thought it was."

We stopped talking for a moment as, two rows ahead, Nicole, who's a freshman, lifted up her hair to show the sixth graders her infected ear piercing.

"I don't get it," said Jaz. "You have hundreds of songs. You showed me them. In your book."

For the record, I hadn't shown her. She'd gone into my bag and found them, but oh well.

"Yeah, but the next one has to be drop-dead incredible, or everyone will say I'm a one-hit wonder, and I'll just be this complete has-been for the entire rest of my life. And with 'Just Me,' it was like I wrote it without even thinking about it, and it somehow came out all right. But now the more I think about it, the less I can do anything. It's like, everything that happens to me, I'm saying, 'Is that a song?' and so it never is."

"Why can't you use one of the ones you already have?"

"Tony didn't like any of them." It was the first time I'd said it out loud. "We had this big meeting, and I played him tons of stuff, and he kept saying the songs didn't work."

"Even 'Cake Boyfriend'?"

"Even 'Cake Boyfriend.' And then when I got home I had this email. Hold on…" I found it and showed her, being sure to keep my fingers firmly wrapped around the screen.

Katie!

Great meeting.

Loved revisiting your back catalog! You are such a talent.

Our feeling is that you should try to write a brand-new single.

Possible themes:

- *A song about partying. Please, no references to anything inappropriate.*
- *A song about first love. Please, no references to anything inappropriate.*
- *Something about animals. Maybe cats? People on social media love cats. Do you have a cat? If not, we can loan you one.*

Hope that has you feeling inspired! If you want to run any ideas by me, my door is always open!

Looking forward to
hearing from you.
Tony

"So he wants a song about going to a party where you fall in love with a cat," said Jaz.

"Yeah."

"I wouldn't mind hearing that," said Jaz unhelpfully.

"Don't hold your breath," I said, wondering if I felt kind of sick because of our conversation or just from reading my phone while sitting on the top deck of a bus. "I'll have to come up with something soon, but I don't know what it'll be." Then: "Sorry, are you okay there?"

I was starting to suspect Jaz wasn't completely focused on what I was saying, on account of how she had my phone (Again? How?) and was frantically typing.

"Jaz!"

"It's all right. I'm not logged in as you."

"Can't you use yours?"

"I'm out of data."

I looked to check she really wasn't logged in as me—because that really would have been a major disaster—and then said, "What are you doing?"

"Giving Nicole's troll the smackdown."

"Nicole has a troll?"

"Yeah," said Jaz, her fingers a blur. "Every time she posts a video, he pops up from his troll hole and tells her she stinks."

"What's she been posting?"

"How she had her wart frozen off." Jaz finished whatever she was typing and tossed my phone into my lap. I picked it up and had a look. There was Nicole's video, paused on a picture of her elbow, which I decided I wouldn't examine too carefully.

Then, underneath, a bunch of likes, a few thumbs-down, and people like Devi and Fin and Paige saying things like "Ugh!" and "Way cool, Nicole" and "So gross I luv it." That was followed by approximately a hundred and twenty posts, all from someone called "sampand45xcg1," saying:

Harltree scum

and

THE WORLD DOES NOT NEED YOU

and

u r a disgusting cow

And so on and on and on.

It was kind of upsetting. And I say that as someone who finds Nicole a little bit disgusting too.

Jaz picked at the lace on her scarf as I tried to imagine what it would be like to be on the receiving end of something so harsh. Tried and failed. In the end, I decided I would never put anything out there that would get anyone quite so worked up.

"It's weird that they've latched on to Nicole," I said. "Maybe she should just stop posting stuff. Or ignore them. It's just words; it's not like it matters."

Jaz gave me a "Jaz" look, which reminded me that Jaz

is really very scary sometimes, and that even though she and I were on fairly good terms at the moment, it was probably better if I continued being a little bit careful in her company.

It also made me think that any troll who dared take her on would be a total idiot, because while a troll is a troll, Jaz is Jaz.

Meanwhile, IRL, Nicole was squirting white junk out of her ear, and Finlay was burping up his breakfast and trying to make us guess what he'd eaten, which made me feel sicker than ever.

So I shut my eyes and lay back, and I tried and failed to think of a song.

Chapter Five

TAKE IT FROM ME, YOU don't want to be doing English homework and simultaneously trying to write a world-conquering hit single. Unless, maybe, the hit single is about English homework, but I sent the idea to Tony and got a single-word reply. A word that began with an *n* and ended with an *o*.

Still, at least I had my best friend to turn to for support. "I am so stressed right now," I said.

We were digesting a particularly grim school lunch, I'd just finished a guitar lesson, and we were sitting on the radiators along the top floor hallway. It's nice up there. The radiators mean it's warm even in winter, and there's a really good view. Only of the parking lot, but still, a parking lot is better than a brick wall. Which is about as much as you can see from the lower hallway, where we'd sat in sixth grade.

It was sad that I knew without even having to ask that Tony wouldn't let me release a song about hallways.

"What's there to be stressed about?" said Lacey, who was rocking a particularly breezy look. She'd clipped her bangs back and rolled down her sock to display the bronze ankle bracelet we'd found on our last trip to the thrift store. "Chill out. It's summer, babes."

"*Babes?*" I repeated. "*Babes* is a Savannah word."

"Well, anyway, it's summer," said Lacey. "Which is the least stressful time of year."

"Unless you have a sunburn."

"I don't get sunburnt."

"Or chafing," I said.

"I told you, stick some talc in there."

"And tests."

"I'm not thinking about that."

"Then what about wasps, Lacey? I can just about maybe believe you're not as sweaty as I am and that maybe your epic-level test denial is keeping you from freaking out, but you have an extreme phobia of wasps!"

"I'm over it."

This did not seem likely, since, last year on field day, Lacey had been chased by a wasp in the four-hundred-meter race and had set a new school record. Which was really something, given that she hadn't even been in the race.

"I thought we were all about winter," I said. "You know. With the Christmas carols and pies. And big coats!"

"Savannah says I've got a great back," said Lacey. "You can't show off your back in a big coat."

I took a moment to consider Lacey's back. From what I could remember, it was just a normal back. Which I told her.

"Actually," said Lacey, looking a little offended, "Sav says it's way better than average. I don't have pimples or back fat, and my shoulders are this perfect ratio to the rest of me. I'm thinking I might go backless to the school dance. Show it off a little."

"Right."

"Katie, are you being unsupportive of my back?"

"No. I love your back. I'm its biggest fan. Second biggest, after Savannah."

"Good."

There was a silence. "We have so much work right now," I said. "I just feel like however much I do, I should be doing more."

"Then why aren't you working now?" Lacey wanted to know. "You could go to the library."

Which wasn't the point. "It's the *idea* of working that I find so hard. It's all this invisible pressure."

"Seriously," said Lacey. "If you want to go, I won't stop you."

"Plus, I can't seem to think of a new song. I just spent a

whole entire guitar lesson with Jill trying to come up with something, and nothing happened, and nothing happened, and then I finally had this idea, but when I tried it out, Jill said I was playing the verses of 'Don't Stop Believin'' and the chorus of 'Empire State of Mind.'"

Was it my imagination, or did Lacey very slightly roll her eyes?

It was my imagination. Of course it was. Because then she said, "Let's write one now. We could call it…'By the Radiators.'"

"Er, no."

"'Looking Down into the Parking Lot'?"

"Lace, it's okay. No one wants you to write it for me," I said. And for some reason I couldn't even begin to understand, she twitched and looked away.

I searched around my brain for things to cheer us both up a little. Usually, the inside of my head is like my bedroom floor, filled with interesting items if you can just find them underneath all the junk. Today, though, there was pretty much nothing.

Nothing except for Dad.

Ever since the phone call, the word had been going around my head like a drumbeat.

Dad. Dad. Dad. Dad.

And—well, you get it.

I was desperate to tell Lacey, crazy eager to talk about it with someone who'd understand. Not Mands. She'd been down on Dad ever since he had gone to America, even though he'd had no choice, because work is work, plus, America is awesome.

And telling Mom…well, to be completely honest, I was still working up to that.

But my best friend would understand, wouldn't she? Lacey knew the whole entire history of the divorce. She'd even been lucky enough to witness a couple of the arguments. Which is, I guess, what had stopped me from saying anything so far. Lace completely got it, of course she did, but if there was even a chance that she'd be anything less than totally excited for me, then it wasn't a conversation I was particularly interested in having.

But she would be. Of course she would be. She'd met him. And now she'd be seeing him again. Maybe he'd even take us out for dinner…

"Dad's coming home," I said, just as Lacey said, "Savannah's dad's hiring a pink stretch limo to take us to the Karamel concert."

"What? That is so tacky." Maybe it was better to leave the family stuff for the moment.

"Yeah. And we're getting majorly dressed up first at Paige's house."

"What a hassle."

A group of boys from our class walked by. A group that included Dominic Preston, who is extremely good-looking.

He gave me a smile, and I fell off the radiator.

"Keep walking please. Nothing to see here," said Lacey, picking me up from the floor.

He laughed and continued down the hall.

"Now that *is* an above-average back," I said, dusting off various pieces of hallway dirt that had stuck to my skirt.

"Katie!" said Lacey. "Are you in love with Dominic Preston? Whoa, are you going to ask him to the dance?"

"He is extremely good-looking," I admitted.

"I thought we promised to fall in love at the same time so that we could talk about it together."

We had agreed about this when we were eleven, and falling in love had been as academic as something that was actually academic, like trigonometry. I think we'd even pinkie promised, which is embarrassing, partly because I don't like to break that kind of thing, and also, pinkie promises are extremely cringeworthy.

"I cannot control my heart," I told Lacey.

"So you *are* in love with him! That is *so* unfair! Who am I supposed to fall in love with?"

"You're basically in love with Savannah," I mumbled.

"What?"

"I don't know. Um, Devi Lester? Finlay? You could totally go to the dance with Finlay."

"Finlay smells like pickled onion rings."

"And do you find that attractive in a guy?"

"No!"

I did, for a second, wonder what it was that I found attractive in Dominic Preston and whether I really was in love with him. There was his extremely good-looking face, of course, a sort of biggish nose and gray-blue eyes. And his mouth was the right size for a mouth. Not small, like Finlay's, with his little nibbly rabbit teeth. And not huge and flappy, like Devi Lester's. Kissing Devi Lester would be genuinely hazardous. He'd probably get most of your face in there. You'd be at risk of losing your chin. Kissing Dominic Preston, though… What would that be like? He was a smiley kind of a person, so it would maybe be really fun. Probably he'd make a joke, and then I'd laugh and he'd smile.

Having him get really close, though…maybe even sticking his tongue in my mouth…hmm. I probably did want him to, but not as much as I wanted the green suede sling-back pumps I'd seen last week at River Island.

Because…unlike the sling-back pumps, which were definitely amazing, kissing Dominic Preston might be, well, a little yucky. Not having kissed anyone before, it was hard to know what to expect. And when it comes to kissing, there are so many things to worry about.

Suppose it turns out that he doesn't ever brush his teeth? Suppose he leans in and I feel sick and I'm trapped in the kiss and I end up barfing into his open mouth?

I mean, I've never heard of it happening before, but there's a first time for everything.

A rush of sixth graders let us know that it wasn't too long before the end of lunch, so we gathered up our stuff.

And Lacey said, in the most casual possible way, so casual that she made sure to look at her bag rather than me, "You sure you don't want to come to Karamel with us?"

"You're deigning to invite me to come to something that you're only going to because I gave you tickets in the first place?"

"Huh?"

"I mean, how can *you* invite *me*, when the whole thing was my idea? That's just…wrong."

The bell rang, and I followed her down the stairs.

"It's just, I know what you'll be like," said Lacey.

"What's that supposed to mean?"

"You'll get into one of your moods and sit around in your room and listen to something angry like Utopia—"

"Nirvana."

"Yeah, them. And you'll be all touchy and not

answer your phone and spend the next week giving me these looks."

We stopped outside our classroom.

"I do not recognize the person you are talking about," I said. "If you want to waste a perfectly good evening watching the world's worst band, then fine. But I have other things to do. I mean, boy band? Boy bland, more like."

"See?" She turned around and headed inside to her desk. "You're doing it already!"

And before I could reply, Sofie and Paige came floating over in a cloud of Vera Wang Princess.

"Message from Savannah," said Paige. "We've got to go long. Legs are so out. Do you have anything maxi?"

"But my legs are my best feature!" said Lacey.

"I thought your back was your best feature," I said.

She made a face. And then, "Can I borrow your blue dress?"

"No."

"It's for one night."

"I'm using it," I said.

"Fine. I'll just have to go shopping."

"Ooh, can I come?" said Paige.

"Yes!" said Lacey. "Are you free tonight? We could go to Cindy's, get some ideas."

"I have dance tonight. When's the concert?"

"The ninth," said Lacey. "So I guess we could go tomorrow. Or…"

"The *ninth* of *July*," I said. "That date sounds sort of familiar, doesn't it, Lace?"

"Does it?"

"Yes. Are you sure it's not ringing any bells with you?"

She thought for a second. "Nope. God, Katie, why are you being so weird? If you want to come, come!"

And in my head I was screaming, *I don't want to come! What I want is for you to realize it's my birthday that night and to say of course you'd rather hang out with me, and maybe at the same time you could admit Karamel is a bad band, and Savannah and co. are annoying, and perhaps you could stop with all the leg and limo chat while you're at it!*

Even Nirvana wouldn't be angry enough for this.

Happy birthday, dear Katie.
Happy birthday to me.

IT'S IMPORTANT I HAVE THAT there because *no one else sang it.*

To be fair, Mom did at least have a present waiting on my plate when I finally staggered downstairs. (A pair of earrings with real diamonds in them! Teeny-weeny ones, but still!)

And Adrian had gotten me the reissue of *Frank* on vinyl, which was waiting in a flat, shiny box next to my seat, underneath birthday cards from Gran and Auntie Tasha, who isn't a real auntie. She's Mom's friend from nursing school, but hey, it's always good to have an extra auntie.

"Do you like it?" said Adrian, his early-morning face sporting a light coating of silver-and-black stubble.

I ripped off the paper. "Yes! Yes, I do!"

He did a whole playing-the-drums mime thing and ended with a *ba-doom-tish*.

Now, me and Adrian had had our ups and downs recently, pretty steep ups and downs, come to think of it, what with him being Mom's new boyfriend and my self-appointed manager. And he had a bad habit of coming downstairs in the mornings wearing Mom's flowery bathrobe.

Still, things had been getting better. And it was sweet that he cared so much about making me happy.

Yeah. Adrian was okay.

Amanda had been in the bathroom when I woke up and in the bathroom while I got dressed. She'd still been in there when I banged on the door and said I had to brush my teeth and do certain other things, quite urgently. She'd still been in there when I'd gone to do them in the downstairs bathroom, which I try to avoid at all costs, because there's a serious risk that people in the kitchen might overhear.

When she finally came in, she was holding something behind her back.

"Happy birthday, K-Star. Fourteen! Sorry I wouldn't let you into the bathroom. I was doing…this."

She handed me a package covered in about twenty different layers of tissue paper and tied with a bunch of swirly ribbons.

"Mands," I said. "Please don't tell me that you've spent the morning wrapping up poop."

She laughed. "Come on. Open it!"

So I did…and…

"Well?" Her eyes were all glowy. "What do you think?"

There in front of me was a brand-new leather-covered notebook, with my name on the front in letters that had been sort of pushed into the leather. And next to it, a pen in a little box.

"It's for your songs!" said my sister. "I know you're always trying to write in that ratty old notebook, so I thought this might inspire you!"

No…no, no, no.

I mean, it was gorgeous. It had the new leather smell that, in the normal way of things, I can't get enough of. And the cover was buttery soft. Then inside, page after pristine page of thick, creamy-white paper.

But if I couldn't write in just my normal lyric book, which was a battered, cardboard-covered thing, how on earth was I supposed to come up with something good enough to put onto these perfect pages?

It deserved someone so much better.

"This is…beautiful," I managed about ten seconds after I should've said it.

"Good," she said. "I'm so glad I found something you can use."

She knew from my face that I couldn't use it.

"It must have been expensive," I said.

"It was."

"Thank you so much."

"All right," said Amanda.

"So, Katie, what's the plan for your party tonight?" said Adrian. "I can go to the grocery store on the way back from the shop. Just tell me what you need."

"Okay," I said. "A tub of Häagen-Dazs, any flavor you like as long as there's no fruit in it—I do not want my happiness being ruined by anything even approaching a vitamin—plus Twinkies and Diet Coke…no wait, not diet, not today."

"Enough sugar to send you to an early death—got it," said Adrian. "And how many pizzas? Is that Savannah girl going to be coming?"

"She's not coming," I said. "And"—this was surprisingly hard to say—"neither is Lacey."

"Not coming to your birthday? Why not?"

"Because they're going to a Karamel concert," I said, feeling really very bleak. "It's my fault. I got them tickets."

Mom started to ask some probably very sensible question, so I held up my hands. "Just…don't."

"So it'll be you and Amanda?"

"I dunno. I mean, I had this whole night planned, with NOW albums one to thirty-seven and dancing and stuff. But if Lacey's not going to be there, it's just you and me, Mands." I sighed. "You probably won't want to…"

Which was Amanda's cue to say that of course she wanted to, that we didn't need Lacey, that my big sis would be looking out for me, making absolutely sure that even though things had gone a little bit wrong, my birthday would still be completely great.

"Well, if you're not interested," said Amanda, fiddling with a piece of abandoned tissue paper. "Maybe we should forget it for this year."

What? No!

"I mean, you're getting a little old to dance around in your bedroom anyway, aren't you?"

No, no, no!

"I guess so," I said.

"Okay then," said Amanda.

It was interesting, because as I was unwrapping my earrings, I thought I'd never be unhappy again. Now, less than twenty minutes later, I was.

And that, ladies and gentlemen, was my special day.

Oh, no, wait—I missed the whole other middle part. Probably because I've been trying to block it out.

I did consider taking a sick day, but I knew Lace would have something special planned. And since I wasn't seeing her that evening, I thought I should let her make a big deal about me during the day.

My uplifting birthday breakfast meant I was running really late. So late that even though I got ready in double-quick time, I had to run if I wasn't going to miss the bus. Running is hard work, especially now that I'm getting older.

"Happy birthday, by the way," said Jaz as we took our places, her in the back seat, and me wheezing and sweating in the next row up—because, while I aspire to be a back-seat person, I don't think I'm there quite yet.

"Thanks," I said, slightly surprised that she even knew about it.

"So"—Jaz folded herself up, her boots completely defying the sticker that said *Please Keep Your Feet off the Seats*—"what does Katie do to celebrate her birthday?"

"I, um, have a dance party," I said, worrying a little that Jaz would think I was a complete child, but somehow it was too early in the morning to think of a decent lie. "Me and Mands and Lacey all jump around to some vintage pop. Well, that's what I normally do. Only, this year…" I trailed off. "That's what I normally do."

Jaz considered the supreme patheticness of a Katie Cox dance party.

"That sounds bearable. What time?" Jaz? At my dance party?

"Um, it's not really…a you kind of thing. It's more for me and Lacey and Amanda. You know."

"Yeah, I know," repeated Jaz, staring out the window as though she was bored to death, which she probably was.

Then, because I hadn't been taking the bus for very long, and it's important to find out this stuff, I asked, "Do you guys have any special birthday rituals I should know about?"

"Like what?"

"Well, if it was your birthday, we used to do this thing where you got thrown into the canal."

"Oh. Right. No," said Jaz. "I mean, we couldn't do that on the bus anyway."

"No," I said. "It would have to be something humiliating but nonmessy. I guess we could draw all over someone with eyeliner. You'd have to hold them down first, but—" I stopped myself. "*Or* we could just be nice to whoever's birthday it is. Like normal people."

"Nah," said Jaz. "Hey, you guys." She was talking to the sixth graders. "Hold Katie down, okay? And, Nicole, get your eyeliner."

♪ ♬ ♫

"Happy birthday," said Lacey as I arrived in the classroom, my face wet and covered with tiny flecks of toilet paper, plus quite a lot of Nicole's eyeliner.

"Thanks, BFF," I said, settling down at my desk. Then, in a whisper, I said, "Um, Lacey? Just how bad do I look right now?"

"Pretty bad," said Lacey. "Your face is gray and splotchy and covered with pieces of white stuff—what is that? And your bangs are all over the place. Why?"

I pretended to examine my fingernails. "Because Dominic Preston is *looking at me*."

Lacey peered over her bag. "He is," she said. "You should smile or something. Look casual. But interested. And happy."

"Like this?"

"What are you even doing with your mouth?"

"This is my casual-interested-happy smile," I hissed.

"Never make that face again. Never, never, never."

"Hey, Katie," said Dominic. "You okay?"

"Yes!" I shouted.

"Okay," said Dominic, and then he went back to talking to Devi.

Me and Lace started to giggle.

"He is so into you," said Lacey. "Don't forget me once the two of you are going out."

"I don't think that's very likely."

"Well, maybe this'll help you remember," said Lace. She reached into her bag and came out holding a little wrapped box.

"Ooh," I said, jiggling it around, then picking it open. "Ooh…a charm bracelet! Lace!"

"They just got them at Samuel's," said Lacey, looking extremely pleased with herself. "I got four charms: a guitar. That's because of how you play the guitar…"

"An ice cream cone!"

"And a microphone, and one of those squiggly things you get on music sheets."

"A treble clef?"

"If you say so."

"Aw, Lace," I said, thinking I might cry. And then really wanting to, because it would show her how happy I was. Which meant, of course, that my eyes immediately dried up again. "It's beautiful."

"I tried to get something to be our Chinese takeout, but they only had this Chinese-symbol one, and I didn't know what it meant, so I thought I'd better not."

"Yeah," I said. "Like the one that Karamel lead singer has on his arm. I bet it means 'I am a butt-face.' Like, why have a tattoo in a language you don't understand?!"

"Um." She looked away. "I realized, last night…the concert, your birthday…talk about bad timing."

Thank the Lord.

"Yeah," I said.

"Why didn't you just tell me?"

"Because I didn't want to spoil your amazing fun night with Savannah and co."

"But if you'd said something at the time…" She was looking at me, her face all open and kind. "Katie, I feel terrible."

"It's okay!" I insisted. "I have it all planned out! We're going to have our regular dance party. Unfortunately Mands is unavailable, but that just means extra pogoing space, and Mom and Adrian said we can make as much noise as we like."

"Yay! It's going to be terrific, Katie. We'll bust some moves and have Coke and pizza and ice cream—whatever you want. Plus, I've got this major new lip stuff we need to try. It puffs up your mouth like crazy. You can't even get it in stores—it's that good."

I fastened the bracelet around my wrist. "I knew you'd understand, Lace. You're the best friend ever."

"Compliment accepted," said Lacey. "And the good thing about doing it tomorrow is that we have extra time to look forward to it."

"Um…tomorrow? But I thought…you would… cancel…because…"

Her expression made me stop.

"Katie, I can't back out now. I promised Savannah. She booked a limo!"

"Oh…okay." It came out a little wobbly.

She put her hand on my arm and looked me right in the face. "Katie, it's just twenty-four hours."

"It's fine," I said. Translation: *It is not fine.*

Lacey speaks fluent Katie. Or I thought she did. "And I'm going to text you from the concert."

"Cool." Translation: *Please don't.*

"And I'll be thinking of you tonight. Thanks so much for the tickets."

"No problem. Just going to run to the bathroom before French." Translation: *I am about to burst into tears.*

Chapter Seven

S O THAT WAS IT, REALLY. Katie's Birthday Spectacular.

By the time I got up to my bedroom—after a special dinner, hand-cooked by Adrian, of slightly-past-its-expiration-date ham-and-pineapple pizza and too much Häagen Dazs—I was pretty much over it.

So I crawled into bed and snapped off the light, ready to sleep it off.

It didn't work. Maybe because it was only seven thirty.

Fine. Maybe now was the moment to write that song for Tony.

I pulled my guitar out from underneath my hoodie and…

No. Nothing.

I don't really understand about writing songs.

When it's going well, it's like the music is just there, inside of me, or maybe inside of my guitar, waiting for me to set it free. I don't notice that I'm trying to come up with rhymes or that the chords don't quite fit because time's standing still and also going at triple speed.

It's not an easy thing to explain. All I can say is that although I know I'm working really hard, I don't even notice.

When it's going badly, though…it's like I'm made of the wrong stuff. Like my fingers are someone else's, and the music's all drained out of my guitar, as though words are strange, spiky tools, and I don't know how to use them.

No, that doesn't even begin to cover it. There's this sneaking feeling I get, that I've never really been able to write, that every other song I've come up with was an accident, a fluke, or maybe something I'd stolen without realizing it. It's like when you get insomnia. You know you've gone to sleep before. That every night of your life until now, you just turned over and did it. Only, you can't remember how, and the more you think about it, the more impossible it feels, like someone's asking you to fly or turn invisible.

It's like a part of me died. Or maybe it was never really there in the first place.

Superstar?

Super failure, more like it.

My new phone went *ding!*

And there was a Lacey-Savannah-Paige-Sofie selfie:

four pouty duck faces in front of a gigantic pink limousine, along with the words:

Hey, Katie, we're here!!!

I threw my guitar across the room.

Then I went and picked it up because the evening was going bad enough without me breaking that too.

What was wrong with them? Karamel weren't even slightly decent at the best of times. How could going to see the band be better than spending time with me on my fourteenth birthday?

Ding!

Now they were posing next to a gigantic gold letter *K*.

EXCITED!!!!

Great, Lacey. I am glad that missing my birthday in order to hang out with the band I hate most in the world is making you so very happy.

LOOK! OOOOOH!

And now a photo of the poster filled my screen, three big stupid boy faces with even bigger, stupider boy hair.

Not only were they the worst and most annoying set of people in the actual universe, they were also quite literally ruining my life with their very existence.

Karamel, with their stupid songs about how much they loved their moms and their bandmates and the invisible, imaginary girl standing in front of them.

Karamel, who always seemed to be photographed fooling around on the beach. Or in a swimming pool. Or on a trampoline.

Karamel, who seemed to start every song sitting on barstools.

Karamel, who—

Ding!

OMG K I CANNOT BELIEVE U R MISSING THIS!!!!!!

Another selfie, this time of Lacey looking crazily flushed in front of the stage, with three lit-up blobs in the background. Honestly, the way she was going, she'd run out of exclamation marks.

Ding!

THIS IS THE BEST NITE OF MY LIFE!!!!!!!!!!!!!!!!

And the worst night of mine.

What could I say?

What *was* there to say? And then...

And then...

I found that I had quite a lot of things to say, after all.

> Can't stand the boy band
> Plastic faces, stupid hair
> Can't stand the boy band
> The matching clothes they wear
>
> The tattooed Chinese symbols
> On the skin that's perma-tanned
> I can't stand the boy band

Ding!

IM SO HAPPY RITE NOW THANK U THANK U
THANK U

> Don't like the boy band
> Singing songs about their grans
> Don't like the boy band
> Hanging around their camper vans
>
> Their lyrics are predictable

> Their music's oh so bland
> I don't like the boy band

Maybe this song was already inside me, waiting. Maybe it had spent the last few months growing, feeding on the drip-drip of loathing I'd swallowed every time Savannah professed her undying love for them, or Paige sighed and said, "Swoon."

It certainly felt that way. My guitar seemed to offer up the chords before I even thought of them, and the chorus was right there, as though I was climbing a ladder, and each word was a rung, easy, within reach, leading me up and on.

> Oh poor sweet boy band
> Your music makes me heave
> You poor sad boy band
> Soon one of you will leave
>
> And if you think you'll be remembered
> Then you misunderstand
> RIP the boy band

What had I been so worried about?

Songwriting was easy.

Ding!

Katie, what's the matter?
Tell me what's wrong please

My fingers went to reply.

And then, I thought, No. I can do better than that. If she wants to know, I'll tell her.

I propped my phone up on an empty tissue box and started the voice recorder.

Then I picked up my guitar, and I began to sing.

Can't stand the boy band
Plastic faces, stupid hair…

And as I sang, I got angrier and angrier, until I could almost feel the threads of fire trailing from my fingertips as I slashed at the strings.

So angry, in fact, that by the time I finished, I was a little bit breathless, and I could feel my cheeks pulsing, magma-hot underneath the back of my hand.

Done. Finished.

For a second, I hesitated. After what had happened last time…

Only then, I had thought, *No, it's fine. I'm not sticking it online or anything. I'm not actually crazy. I'm just going to send it to a friend.*

I knew it wasn't my best idea ever. That it would probably cause a fight with Lace. But that was fine. In a slightly twisted way, it's what I wanted.

At least, it was at that precise moment. It probably wouldn't be once I'd had a chance to calm down.

Better send it now then.

Very quickly, before I could change my mind, I opened a new message to Lacey, attached the file, and hit Send.

And then…then I somehow felt a little flat.

The song must have gotten all the angry stuff out of my system, like when you pop a zit and what was tight and inflamed before goes back to normal again, with just a cruddy piece of tissue and a little redness to show that anything was wrong in the first place.

Ding!

Here we go.

I reached for my phone, only then Mom's voice came shouting up the stairs.

"Katie? Something's…Katie! Get down here. Katie? Katie!"

I gulped. It takes a lot for Mom to be freaked out. "Katie! Are you…can you…Katie? Katie, Katie, Katie!" Mom was totally freaking out.

"What is it?" I said, opening my bedroom door and edging across the hallway to peer down the stairs. "What happened?"

"Hello, Katie."

There, standing on the doorstep, surrounded by suitcases, was Dad.

Chapter Eight

OH MY GOD!"

It's hard for me to describe Dad because he's just basically Daddish to me. But if a stranger had been there too, they'd have seen: a smiling man with thick black hair, wearing a gray cotton shirt with the top three buttons undone. Decent jeans and a belt with a big buckle I hadn't seen before, so maybe that was a thing he'd picked up in America. Only, he wasn't in America anymore. He was right in front of me.

"Katie!"

Then I was flying down the stairs and throwing myself into his arms, hugging him so tight that if it was anyone else I would have been afraid of breaking them, but not Dad—Dad who was so tall and real and wonderfully, amazingly *here*.

"This is the best birthday surprise ever!"

"Is it…yes! Happy birthday!"

And we might have stood like that forever, or at least a good couple of minutes, only we were interrupted by Mom saying, "What the hell, Benjamin?"

He stood back, and I saw that he looked tanned and thin…and tired.

Oh, Dad.

"Good to see you too, Zoe."

"You can't just turn up out of the blue like this. I have a life now. You have no right to just waltz back in and—"

He took a step back, puzzled. "But Katie said she'd—"

They both looked at me. "Katie, you said you'd tell her I was coming…?"

"Ah. Um. Yes. Mom, Dad's coming back."

"Katie…I…"

Mom isn't often lost for words. I somehow knew she'd make up for it later.

"Hello, hello? Who is this?"

Adrian came through the hall and stopped.

"This," said Mom, "is Benjamin. My ex-husband."

"Well, he can't stay on the doorstep," said Adrian, sticking out one of his big, thick hands. "Nice to meet you, Benjamin. I'm Ade. Come on in."

Then actual Dad was standing in my actual living room, peering up at the cracks in the ceiling.

"How long have they been there?"

"Since we moved in," I said, just as Mom said: "Couple of days."

He sucked his teeth. "That's not good. You should get someone to come by."

"Thanks for the input, Benjamin," said Mom. "Any other thoughts on our house? While you're here?"

Dad's never been good at picking up sarcasm, and his stint stateside clearly didn't improve matters because he said, "You should knock through that wall and get some light in here. Open things up—you've got the dimensions, but the furniture's too big. It feels cramped. And that's quite a drainage problem in the garden."

Mom's knuckles were turning white. Luckily, Adrian was between them.

"It's a real fixer-upper, that's what it is, Benj. Great to have your views on the place actually. We're still at the ideas stage. Beer?"

"Got any wine open?" said Dad. "A nice Shiraz would just hit the spot."

Adrian tossed him a can of Guinness. Dad caught it,

barely, and we all waited. Then he opened it and sat down on the sofa.

I sat down too. And so did Adrian. Mom stayed standing up.

"So Katie tells me you're a musician," said Adrian. "Must be where she gets it from."

"Yeah, yeah, mainly session work," said Dad. "But it keeps me busy. Just got out of the studio last week. We were doing this huge stint on a new album, all very secret, of course, can't tell you much about it, but let's just say that a certain Miss Alicia Keys will be gracing the airwaves pretty soon with someone you know rather well."

"Really?" I squeaked. "Dad, that is so cool!"

"It's just work," said Dad. "I don't even get excited about it anymore, to be honest."

"You should be excited," I told him.

He gave me a squeeze. "Maybe."

"Adrian is a very successful retailer," said Mom. "He owns Vox Vinyl!"

"It's just a little shop in town," said Adrian.

"He's taking over the space next door," said Mom.

"And then, the world!" said Adrian.

"Great," said Dad. "So, Katie, would you like Alicia's autograph?"

"*Would I?!* Dad, that is so amazing! Best present ever!"

His hand went to his pocket, and I thought my heart might stop then and there. "Thought so. I'll let her know."

He tapped out a quick message, just as I heard the front door open. Amanda.

"We're in the living room," I called.

I could hear her taking off her boots and then the double thump as she tossed them under the stairs. "Any pizza left? Because—uuuuh."

She was in the doorway, and she sort of began to crumple, her hands clutching against the wood as though the sight of Dad had been a punch.

"Dad? What are you…?" She shook her head. "Dad."

He got to his feet, and, I dunno, maybe it was that she was older or that he was thinner, but I saw for the first time the way their hair curled up at the ends, that funny shrug they both do when they're embarrassed, the way their eyes have that little crease, just underneath, in the shadows.

He held out a hand. "Come here, sweetheart."

And what do you know? She burst into tears.

Really long sobs, as Mom and Adrian looked at their feet.

He put his arms around her, and she shook, and I knew exactly how she felt.

"Amanda, angel, it's okay."

She dabbed at her eyes, and then, after I passed her a tissue, her nose.

"How come you're here?"

He looked at me. "Katie, did you tell *anyone* I was coming? Anyone at all?"

I didn't really know what to say, so I just made a face.

"Well, no harm done," said Dad. "I'm here now."

"No harm done?" said Amanda, the tissue dropping to the floor. "*No harm done?*"

"Sorry," I murmured.

"Dad, why didn't you tell me? You know what Katie's like."

"I didn't…we hadn't spoken in a while. So…"

"We hadn't spoken because I can never get you on the phone!" She wiped her nose on the back of her wrist and glared.

"Work's been crazy, and there's the time difference. And I know you have a job now. I can't just call you whenever."

"Yes, you can, Dad," said Amanda.

"Okay then," said Dad. "From now on, I will."

"Great."

There was a long pause. I got to work filling it. "Er, Mands, what do you mean, 'You know what Katie's like'?"

"Oh, you know." She flapped an irritated hand. "Useless."

"What? How can you say that? I'm not the one who bailed on her little sister *on her fourteenth birthday*."

"That is not what we are talking about."

"Then what *are* we talking about?"

This was turning into one of those arguments that you never remember starting and so you can't ever end it.

"Just…shut up, Katie."

Dad took a step forward. "Don't talk to your sister like that."

"Great," said Amanda. "You run off to America, and now you're back, and you're trying to *discipline* me? I'm going to bed."

When she slammed the door, it bounced a few times and then fell off its hinges.

"So," said Dad, who was going for the "Let's Pretend None of That Just Happened" way of dealing with things. "Is someone going to give me a tour?"

"It's late," said Mom. "Maybe you should go…wherever you're staying…and we'll do the tour another time."

This is when it occurred to me that there was another part of Dad's message I'd failed to deliver.

"Well, actually, Mom, I sort of said he could stay here. With us."

Dad did the shruggy, grinny thing that he does. Mom started to inflate.

I went into crash position in my head.

Only then, before she could blow, Adrian nodded.

"Sure you can. Plenty of room in the den, as long as you don't mind a few mushrooms. Want to follow me? I'll get you all set up."

Off they went. "Katie—" Mom began.

"Oh, dear, is that the time? I'm so very tired," I said.

And before she could stop me, I was racing back up the stairs to my room and ignoring Amanda, who was staring out the window at the rain. I pulled my cover over my head and stuck my headphones on my ears, noticing as I did that I had twenty-five missed calls from Lacey.

Was I in the mood to hear how fabulous her evening had been?

No.

No, I was not.

I lay there, in the dark, hearing my breath flutter, in, out, in, out.

Dad was back. Here.

Home.

Maybe it wasn't such a bad birthday after all.

My Dad

My dad rocks hard
My dad is ace
My dad plays lead guitar
And drums and sax and bass

My dad's way cool
My dad's so fine
My dad lives his dream
And shows me mine

Wish I'd seen his stateside pad
Yeah, I bet that place was rad
I'm glad
So glad
He's my dad

My dad was gone
My dad went away
My dad, across the ocean
And the sky turned gray

I think of what we had
And all I feel is sad

But I'm glad
So glad
He's my dad

My dad was lost
My dad's been found
My dad spins the world
With his unique dad sound

My sister says he's bad
And he makes my mother mad
But still, I'm glad
So glad
He's my dad

I'm glad
So glad
He's my dad

Chapter Nine

WAKE UP, K."

I opened my eyes to see a sliver of morning sun, which was being blocked out by Amanda's great big face, so close that I could see the pores all around the edges of her nose. Pores that could use a wash, if we're being honest, which I was about to be, when—

"Can we talk? Or are you going to dive back under your duvet again?"

Diving under the duvet didn't sound half bad, but in the interests of sisterly cooperation, I didn't.

"What do you want to talk about?"

"Dad. He's here. In this house. Downstairs. Right now."

I remembered and grinned, giving Mands an eyeful of my morningy teeth. "Isn't it the best?"

"No," said Amanda. "It isn't. It's the opposite of that. Mom's a wreck. And she said that you told him it would be okay to stay? What were you thinking?"

"I was thinking that it would be nice for us all to be together again," I said.

"So you weren't thinking," said Amanda.

She was trying to look into my eyes, and I thought how strange it was that she couldn't see that this was Dad we were talking about. Our dad. Mine and hers. How strange and how sad.

If she didn't understand this, then really, there was nothing else to say.

So I broke her gaze and turned away to get dressed.

By the time I finished, she was gone.

Probably for the best, I thought as I went downstairs. And there he was!

"Morning, my darling," said Dad, sitting at the breakfast table and buttering himself a cinnamon bagel.

"Morning!" I sang, giving myself a celebratory double helping of Cocoa Krispies.

"Morning all," said Adrian. "Um, Zoe said to apologize, but she's on an early shift today, so she'll see you all later."

"I thought her early shift was next week," I said.

"No," said Adrian. "It's today."

"It's definitely next week," I insisted, because it was.

"Avoiding me, is she?" said Dad.

Adrian gave me a look, and I decided I'd shut up for a while.

"Nasty leak you had there," said Dad, nodding at the weird marks on the ceiling above the fridge. "You'll want to get that repaired."

"Yup, it's on the list," said Adrian, and I guess it was because it was so early that he sounded a little bit exhausted.

Dad went back to his bagel for a while. Then, he said, "Hey, Katie, want a lift to school?"

"Total yes!" I thought about it for a second. "Do you have a car? Already?"

"Nah, I'll take Adrian's. You don't mind. Do you, Ade? Give us a chance to do some father-daughter bonding."

"But you're not insured, *Benj*."

Dad gave him a playful smack in the stomach. "Just this once."

"But—"

"Oh, go on," I said. Because, really, a chauffeured ride to school with Dad versus a bus trip watching Nicole waxing her arm hair with duct tape—it wasn't much of a contest.

Adrian made a grab for the kitchen counter, but Dad's hand was already there. Then Dad was holding up the car keys.

"Ready when you are, Katie."

So we whizzed past the bus stop and zoomed along by the fields, and Dad drove far too fast, and it was awesome. And then, way too soon, I was getting out at the drop-off by school and heading for the classroom, with a whole six hours before I'd see him again.

"Katie," said Lacey, staggering in and plunking herself down into her chair. "Why aren't you answering your phone?"

I wrenched my mind back from the Amazing Dad Show and tried to focus. "I've been…very…busy."

"You're sulking about your birthday, aren't you? I knew you would, and you are."

"Am I?"

"Honestly, Katie, get over it."

"I'm over it," I said. Then, as I really digested what she'd said, "It's been kind of a mess at home, that's all."

"Ri-iiight." Lacey folded her fingers under her chin and sighed, and I gradually became aware she was waiting for me to ask her something.

I wasn't sure what, so I just said, "So…what's the…you know…?"

Lacey sighed. "The concert was just…" She searched for the right word. "Like…I mean, when they sing, Katie. I thought I'd die. Honestly, I did. We were in the middle of the front row, and when Kurt did 'Beautiful Girl,' he looked straight at me and—"

"Ah," I said as it all came back to me, like a boomerang comes back and smacks you in the face. "Karamel."

"Yes, Karamel."

Now that I was remembering, I preferred it when I'd forgotten.

"I cried," said the idiot who had apparently taken possession of my best friend. "I actually cried."

"Right."

"When you see them, live, it's…it's…" She shivered. "I'm shivering just thinking about it."

"Maybe you should go see the nurse."

"So, afterward, we went backstage—we had these wristbands that they gave us. I'm never cutting mine off!"

She waved it at me.

It was just a wristband. "Well go on," I said.

Lacey went on. And on and on. Stuff about dance moves and photographers and after parties and blah-blah-blah-de-blah.

"And then as we were going back to the limo, I listened to that song you sent me, which you clearly wrote just to irritate me, and it *isn't going to work*, all right? We are going to rise above this."

"Are we?"

"Katie, I know you have Karamel issues, but it was the best night of my life. So thank you for getting me the ticket, and I'm sorry it clashed with your birthday. There. That's it. Over. Okay? And did you find anything at all to say about that poem because I didn't, and I basically wrote a whole page about nothing, and English is next, and I'm worried McAllister will notice."

The bell rang.

And I saw that I had a choice. I could continue being annoyed, or I could do the sensible thing and try to move on.

Or I could *pretend* to move on while being secretly still a little annoyed, which is what I decided I'd do, because when someone offers you the Hand of Friendship, you have to take it, or they'll just hate you forever.

"Okay," I said. "It's over."

She nodded. "Good. Now, what do you mean, it's all been a mess at home?"

"Dad's back," I said, and hearing myself say the words was kind of a relief. Because while, obviously, as far as Dad was concerned, everything was 100 percent positive and completely fine, it was all getting a little complicated. And it might be useful to say everything out loud and untangle it with someone who cared about me. Yes, it would be good to double-check with Lacey that everything was as totally all right as I definitely knew that it was.

"Your dad? Whoa. Has there been major drama?" Lacey did this exaggerated frowny face. "No wonder you've been so grumpy."

"Minor drama," I said. Then, because that wasn't quite true, I said, "I mean, medium-level drama. Anyway, the point is…"

Only, I never got to tell Lacey what the point was because Savannah came drifting up and put her arm around Lacey's shoulders, drawing her away.

"Hi-hi."

For someone who'd stayed out very late at a celebrity party, Savannah was looking surprisingly fresh, her hair somehow glossier than usual, and even her eyelashes curled to perfection. Maybe she didn't undress after she got home, but just climbed into some kind of Barbie packaging and slept standing up.

"Katie, have you *heard*?"

"Heard what?"

"Amaze," said Savannah.

"What?" I said. "Spit it out. We have to get to English."

"Should I tell her?" said Lacey, as though I wasn't even there.

"No, I'll do it," said Savannah. "Katie. Are you ready? Because this changes everything."

I was finding it very hard to be the chilled-out person I usually am. "What changes what?"

"I'm going out with Kolin. From Karamel. Kolin from Karamel."

"Oh, right," I said.

This was clearly not the reaction Savannah had been expecting.

"I am going out with Kolin from Karamel."

"Yes, I get it."

"She doesn't care," said Lacey. "You know how she feels about them. It's like she's missing part of her brain or something."

"Or you are," I murmured.

Savannah didn't show any sign of having heard me. "So after the show, we all go to the party, and I can feel someone looking at me. And it's him! It's Kolin! And we talked and talked, and it turns out we like tons of the same things, and then he gave me his number, and I gave him mine, and now he's my boyfriend."

"That's great, Savannah," I said. "You two sound perfect for one another. You like Karamel. He's in Karamel. It's a match made in heaven."

Once, Lacey would have laughed. Now, she said, "Maybe it is."

Then the two of them fell into step ahead of me,

Savannah's gold-plated phone glinting between them like a stupid expensive phone that had been covered in stupid expensive gold.

"Our pics have been getting some major play," Savannah said. "Like, *major* major."

"Wow," said Lacey.

I dropped back a little. They'd probably slow down and wait for me.

"Oooooh, Kol posted the twinkle-lights one! I am so glad he is my boyfriend."

"Yay, me too!"

It was almost as though they preferred to talk to each other than to me!

"Oof, the Karamel fans are sooooo jealous," said Savannah. "Total eeek. I'd probably better change my profile name."

"And maybe not have your avi be the one of you kissing Kolin," said Lacey.

"Let's not go crazy," said Savannah. "I mean, I'm, like, not going to let the haters control my life, you know? Just because I am lucky enough to have someone from a very major band as my boyfriend. I cannot live a lie."

"No," said Lacey. Then: "Oh no. No, no, no."

"No! Nooooooo!"

They stopped and turned, and a very pathetic part of me actually felt grateful for a little eye contact.

"Katie," said Lace. "You need to see this."

Savannah held up her phone.

It was the feed from *Kurt_Karamel*.

"No," I said. "I do not want to hear about last night anymore."

"K! This is important!"

"It's not! It's really not."

"Um, actually, Katie…"

"How are we still talking about this?" I said in this sort of shriek. "Yay, you went to see Karamel. Woo, you partied backstage. Squee, Kolin and Savannah are now an item. I'm. Not. Interested."

"Is she okay?" said Savannah. "She doesn't seem okay. Katie, are you okay?"

"I'm *fine*," I said. "But I would be even more fine if we could just talk about something else."

People were stopping and turning around. "Look at it, Katie." Lacey's voice was serious.

"No!"

"You have to look!"

"*No!*"

"*Katie, you have to read this.*"

"Why?"

"*Read it.*"

The screen was right in front of my eyes, and I focused long enough to see:

Kurt_Karamel:

Hey there.
Found out about this last night.
Kinda upset as I was a big fan of hers
Peace and love
Kurt x

And underneath was a link.

The phone began to sing in my voice:

Can't stand the boy band…

Kurt had posted my song.

Chapter Ten

"**H**A HA HA HA HA," said Jaz. "You insulted Karamel. Ha ha ha ha ha ha ha ha ha. Ha ha ha ha ha ha ha ha ha."

There was quite a lot more of this, but it's way boring written down.

We were on the bus because despite promising me a ride home—"While I'm around, my princess will not be using public transportation"—Dad had failed to materialize. I'm guessing Adrian had wanted his car back, which is kind of selfish.

Anyway, Jaz and I were in the back, watching Nicole trying to hack some false nails from her fingers.

"She didn't realize you have to pay to get them taken off again," said Jaz as Nicole attacked them with the end of a compass.

The bus went over a bump, and I looked away. The windows were smeary on the inside, and the outsides were coated with these vague gray spots of yuk.

Then a cheer. "First one's off!" said Fin.

"Great!" I said, hoping there hadn't been too much collateral damage.

Then Jaz remembered about the Karamel thing again. "But how did he get ahold of the song? I thought you only sent it to Lacey."

"I did," I said, a tiny area of my brain registering that Jaz sounded a little hurt, but really, there was no time for that now. "I sent it in a private message."

"Then how did he…?"

I thought back to that terrible moment a couple of hours earlier, as we all stood outside the English room, staring at each other.

"Lace, did you send it to Kurt?"

"Of course I didn't!" said Lacey. "How could I?" Long pause.

"I did send it to Sofie, though. It was too noisy to hear it in the limo, so she wanted to listen when she got home."

We all turned to Sofie.

"I only sent it to Devi Lester," she said.

"How did Devi Lester…? Why Devi Lester? And how did it get from Devi to—"

"Okay, that would be me." Paige let out this fluttery laugh. "So Devi has this really fun messenger group. It's so fun, Katie, you should get him to add you. Anyway, he has this group, and whenever he finds something fun, he shares it, and normally it's

just Nicole squeezing zits or whatever, but this time, it was you, which is fun, so Devi sent it out, and I saw it, and I was all, like, 'Ooooh' and I kind of sent it to Mom because she's a fan of yours."

"Yeah," said Jaz, who was clearly starting to get a little bored with this story. "So that's how it got from Devi to Paige's mom. But how did it go from Paige's mom to Kurt from Karamel?"

"I'm getting to that," I said. "So, Paige's mom, apparently, sent it to Cindy, you know Cindy? She runs that shop, in town. Cindy's. And Cindy sent it to…"

"Savannah."

Savannah looked up from her phone and smiled.

"What?"

"Savannah, did you send Kurt from Karamel an MP3 of Katie being stupid?"

"No!" said Savannah.

"Then, how…?"

"I sent it to Kolin!" She applied a little bit of Lancôme juicy tube and smacked her lips. "He's my boyfriend."

I was brought back to reality by a bunch of Jaz cackles.

"It's not *that* funny."

"Isn't it?" said Jaz.

"Lacey's ready to kill me. And what about all their fans? I'm probably going to have to sleep with a baseball bat by my bed. And—"

"Katie, calm down. These are people who like Karamel." Jaz tried not to smile and failed. "I guess they might *snuggle* you to death…"

"Seriously, though. I was thinking, if I call Tony, he can get them to take it down and maybe we can get the police on it or something, I mean, it's stealing, isn't it? Sticking someone's song online without permission. Isn't it?"

For a second, she actually looked reasonably serious. "Seriously? I've listened to it, and I like it."

"What! When?!"

"Just now. While you were talking." She lifted up her hair to show an earbud, nestling deep in her ear.

"Oh."

"And I think it's cool."

Not that I was especially out to impress Jaz. But… "Do you?"

"Yeah," said Jaz. "I do."

I stared at Jaz's face and thought how different she and Lacey were. With Lace, I know completely what she looks like, how she has a pointy chin and milky skin and freakily tiny ears. Jaz's face, even though I saw it every day, was still kind of a mystery, with its hugely penciled brows and lumps of covered-up zits and angles of cheekbone that seemed to change according to her mood or my mood or the weather or maybe according to how much blush she was wearing.

And she thought my song was cool. We'd reached my stop. So I got off.

♪ ♫ ♫

With a house as vibrant and ever changing as ours, there's always something new to enjoy. Last week there'd been the windowsill underneath Mom and Adrian's bedroom falling off and landing on top of the porch. That weekend, Adrian had hacked away some of the ivy around the side, revealing that part of the house we'd thought had been made of bricks was actually just scraps of lumber held together by a few rusty nails and half a "For Sale" sign from 1996.

And today, there was a huge black car parked outside. Huh.

I took a couple of deep breaths and then went in. To see Tony Topper, head of Top Music, sitting next to Dad, in our living room, being handed a cup of tea by Adrian.

"Hi," I said. "Would you like some tea? Hold on. You have tea. Would you like a cookie?" *Stop talking, Katie.* "We only have sugar cookies, and they're mostly crumbs because I dropped the shopping bag."

Tony very sensibly ignored all this and just said, "Katie, I hope you're well."

He was so sharp and tanned that he made everything

else seem sort of insubstantial somehow. Like he was an actor, and our house was a film set, and if you gave the walls a push, they'd tip over.

Which, come to think of it, they probably would.

"I come bearing good news," he said, smiling with his white, white teeth. "You're aware of the Teen Time Awards?"

"With the poppy bands and the cheesy presenters and the pathetic embarrassing concert at Wembley that's supposed to be spontaneous, but everyone knows is rigged and rehearsed, and the speeches that are always really heart-felt and sappy and basically make me want to puke?"

"Yes," said Tony. "That. You've won a Teen Time Award."

"God, I hate them so much... Did you say I won?"

"Yes. The People's Act. The people voted, and they picked you."

"Whaaaaaaaaaaaat?" If I'd been in a film, it would have done that thing where the background rushes past, and my face goes super close up. "I *won* an *award*?"

"You won the People's Act Teen Time Award, yes."

"*I won?*"

"Yes."

"*I can't believe I won!*"

"Well, you did."

"*That's unbelievable!*"

"Believe it."

"*I can't!*"

Tony turned to Adrian. "Is she all right?"

"In my experience," said Adrian, "this might go on for a while. You can sometimes jolt her out of it by offering her a slice of pizza."

I calmed down. "It's just, I don't win things. I'm not a winning kind of a person. Like"—I tried to explain—"if there's a raffle, say, I just know that I won't pick the right number. I physically can't. The winning tickets see my fingers coming, and they recoil."

"Maybe," said Tony, taking a delicate sip of tea. "But this involved people casting votes. So it's not chance."

"Huh," I said. "Huh."

"The results stay secret until the night of the awards, of course, so keep it under your hat. In the meantime, stick the date in your calendar and think about which song you'd like to play. And—Katie? Are you…crying?"

"Sorry, it's just…" I was thinking of all those people, in their bedrooms, watching me and then bothering to vote. It was kind of amazing. "I didn't know how it would feel. To have people love me. It's nice. That's all."

Adrian gave me a pat on the back, and then Dad got up to give me a hug.

"I'm glad you're so pleased," said Tony. "And I have to say, this all bodes very well for your concert next week.

As instructed, we've booked you a nice, intimate venue, a little place in Camden, seats a couple of hundred. Tickets go on sale tomorrow, and there's been plenty of interest. That and your impending award mean you've really got the wind behind you right now."

"Great!" I decided I wouldn't think about the couple of hundred people. Or the performing part. Or, you know, anything.

"There's just one issue." Tony looked for somewhere to put his mug, considered the cardboard box we were using as a coffee table, and then gave up. "We at Top Music were very interested to hear that you'd written and released a song."

"Ah. The song. Yes."

"Katie, you told me, back in the office, that you didn't have any new material."

"Yeah, but—"

"And we'd worked very hard to come up with a list of things for you to write about."

"Yes, but it was—"

"Then, instead, you write"—he wrinkled his nose—"something else."

"I didn't mean for it to get heard by everyone," I said.

"So"—Tony leaned in as though he was talking to a particularly stupid child—"*why did you put it on the Internet?*"

"I didn't! I literally sent it to one friend! My bes—" I stopped myself. "One friend."

"Karamel are the UK's most successful group. They're with Top Music, like you. They are your agentmates. And now I have to sit at my desk and justify to the world why our newest signing has publicly made fun of our biggest act."

"I'm sorry," I said. "I didn't mean to make life difficult for other people. I just wanted to write a good song."

"From now on, I'll decide if it's a good song," said Tony. "We can talk to Kurt. Get that embarrassment taken down. And replace it with…in fact, we've been working on a little something, if you'd like to take a look…"

He handed me a piece of paper, heavy and white, with "Top Music" printed at the top, and my eyes scanned down to:

> Getting late
> Party's starting
> See my friends
> Music's playing

"Well?"

"It's all right," I said, looking into my lap. Then, I don't know why, but it was like Jaz was sitting on my shoulder. Not a full-size Jaz obviously. That wouldn't work at all. A mini Jaz, whispering into my ear. Saying, "I thought it was cool." Jaz liked my song.

"I'm sorry," I said. And then, as tiny invisible imaginary Jaz rolled her eyes, I said, "I mean, not sorry. I am not sorry. I really like the song I already wrote."

Tony had been about to take another sip of tea, but he paused. So I continued.

"It's just, musically, I'm actually pretty pleased with how it came out. It has all this energy. And there's nothing else like it out there, is there?"

"Why do you think that is?" said Tony.

A vision of Lacey and Savannah, swinging up the hallway ahead of me, comparing selfies.

"I'll tell you why—it's because people are afraid to have an opinion. Everyone plays it safe all the time, so no one ever gets upset, and everything sells to the maximum number of people. And you know what? Maybe this has annoyed some dorky Karamel fans. But so what? I believe in my lyrics."

"I see," said Tony.

"Great!" I said.

"Mmm," said Adrian.

"Isn't Katie something?" said Dad. "I wish I could say she got it from me." He grinned around the room. "I mean, I'm a musician myself, so in a sense, she did."

"Is that right?" said Tony distantly.

"Session work, for the last few years. You know how it is."

"Uh-huh."

"In fact, if you ever need anyone, for anything…"

"Sure," said Tony.

Dad was reaching behind the back of the sofa for a guitar. "Happy to give you a quick demo now, if you'd like. Or I can ping you a link. Whatever's easier."

"Um, Benjamin, buddy, I think he's here for Katie," said Adrian.

"It's fine," I said. "Dad's an amazing musician. You should totally listen to his stuff."

Tony held up his hands. "All right! I will!"

Dad relaxed back into his chair.

"So," said Tony. "Just for the record, Katie, I am asking you, one final time, to write a different song. Something positive. Will you do that?"

"But…"

"You said, just now, how nice it was to feel loved. Do you really want to put out a song that's all about hate?"

And for a second, I did think, *Maybe this man has a point*. I mean, he was the head of a humungous record label with all this experience, and there were a lot of Karamel fans. Maybe I could try writing something else. If not about partying all night then maybe about…cats…?

That would make Lacey happy too. A song about cats or dancing or my awesome friends. It would have me back in everyone's good graces. I could be BFFs with Lacey and friends with Savannah and Sofie and Paige, and maybe we'd all ride around in a pink limo, and I could wear tight clothes and love Karamel like everybody else. Top Music would write my songs, and Savannah would pick my clothes, and I'd go on a diet and...

"No," I said. "My next single is 'Can't Stand the Boy Band.' Exactly as I recorded it in my room."

He got to his feet. "All right then. I will do my very best to sell it."

"Thank you," I said, sort of in shock. Had I really *won*?

"Good luck, Katie."

"Thanks! See you soon, Tony."

And then he was out the door and the big black car was sliding away, leaving me and Adrian staring at each other.

"I hope you know what you're doing," said Adrian.

"Can you give me Tony's email address?" said Dad.

Chapter Eleven

DINNER THAT NIGHT SHOULD HAVE been great, what with having everyone around the table together.

Should have been but wasn't.

Mom was shooting evil eyes at me and Dad.

Amanda was ignoring Dad and shooting evil eyes at me. Adrian was giving me worried looks.

I was sending love vibes to Dad and trying to avoid Mom, Adrian, and Amanda altogether. It was doing terrible things to my digestion.

"Can I go up to my room?" I asked. "I need to get ready for Lacey."

Mom looked up. "Lacey?"

"It's my birthday dance party," I said. "My belated birthday dance party."

"Right," said Amanda, in a way that made it clear she wasn't planning on joining us. "Have fun."

"Will do!" I said.

And then, because while I probably could have eaten one more fajita, it might not have mixed well with the dance moves I was planning to throw, I excused myself and went upstairs to prepare the dance floor.

One look down and I decided to give up. We could dance on top of the mess.

Instead, I lay on my bed and waited for the doorbell. And waited.

But it was nice to have a little me time. Get some headspace. Think about the last twenty-four hours.

Think about my new song. Think about what I'd done.

What *had* I done?

I decided I wouldn't think about it.

My thumb went to my phone and hovered over Lacey's face.

What time R U coming? K x

Soz forgot. Am at Paige's. Come over!
We r doing eyebrows and U r totally invited xx

Oh.

So much for my birthday dance party. So much for best friendship.

Not only had she now doubly abandoned my birthday

celebrations, she was leaving me alone in my hour of need! My song was out there, doing its thing, and I was desperate for a little wisdom. Not a trip to Paige's house and an attack on my facial hair.

Which is when it hit me that Lacey was the worst possible person to help me face all this stuff. She would tell me to get rid of "Can't Stand the Boy Band." She'd probably even bring me a Karamel poster to stick over my bed.

There was another option, though. If I was feeling brave.

And yeah. Why not?

Maybe don't think about that, either.

The reply came through almost before I'd hit Send.

On my way
Jazzzzz x

Twenty minutes later, Jaz was propped up against my bed with my laptop open. She'd made herself very much at home, stuffing my pillow behind the small of her back and resting her muddy platform boots right in the center of Amanda's face towel.

I remembered the last time she'd been in my room, with most of my family, and the impromptu jam session that had lead to the release of "Just Me," and locked the door.

"Have you seen the fallout yet?"

"I'm too…" I wanted to say that I was scared. But Jaz didn't need to hear that. So I just said, "No. Not yet. Been really busy."

"Okay then. Here we go."

She typed my name and whistled.

I pulled my sweater over my head, even though I could hear Mom's voice telling me I was going to ruin it. Then, from inside my woolly tent, I said, "Is it bad? It's bad, isn't it? I really upset people. Oh please don't let me get trolled. I can't stand it. Let's call Tony and get him to take it down."

"Katie, look."

"I just…I don't know what I was thinking. Yes, I do. I was upset at Lacey, and this was my way of getting back at her. But it's immature, it's…"

"Wow."

"I'm sorry."

"Don't be," said Jaz. "Really, look."

I stuck my nose out, and then one eye. And…

LOVE IT.

Finally someone is telling the TRUTH

Stand up for real music!!!!!!!!!!!!!

she haz such a nice voice I luv her

will u follow me Katy I am yr biggest fan

go 2 my site for KATIE COX CLIPS music wallpaper
and MORE
Bet Kristian is first one to leave lol

"They like it," said Jaz. "The people of the Internet are on your side. Well, not the Karamel fans—you're going to have to steer clear of them. Stay in your bubble."

"My bubble?"

"You know," said Jaz. "Your corner. The Katie zone. Friends and fans and stuff."

"They honestly like it?"

"They think you rock."

I looked. And, as crazy as it seemed, clearly, they did. "That's unbelievable," I said. "I am in actual shock."

"I don't get you, Katie," said Jaz. "I don't get you at all." Now this, coming as it did from the world's least-gettable person, was a little on the surprising side.

"What don't you get?" I said, letting my other eye come out from under my sweater. And then the rest of me, because being half in and half out of a sweater is both difficult and uncomfortable.

"You write a song because you have something to say. And then, when people start agreeing, you're all, 'Really?' For the sake of your dignity, Katie, at least try to own it."

Which stung.

"What should I do?" I said. "If I'm going to, um, own it?"

"What do you want to do?" asked Jaz.

"Er, nothing?" Wrong answer.

"How's this?" said Jaz, her black nails tapping at the keyboard.

"What? What did you write?" I leaned around her.

KTCoX: Hey Kurt_Karamel thnkx for posting my song. So nice of u ;) xox

"What? Don't say that! Jaz, what is wrong with you? You're out of control."

She gave me one of her looks, and as she did, I considered how a message like this would look, to the world.

It would look as though I was kind of crazy. And cocky. And confident. And cool.

This, I realized, was why I'd invited Jaz over. She went to delete the words, and I held her arm. "Actually, yeah, say that."

She pressed Return, and there it was. I'd said it.

My insides did a little whoosh.

"I mean, it's not like he'll see," I said, as much to myself as to her. "He must get a gajillion messages a minute. He's hardly going to—"

"He replied," said Jaz. "Freak to the beat—Kurt from Karamel has *replied*."

Kurt_Karamel: Thought you were better than this.

We looked at each other, and I became aware that we were both squealing. I mean, not in a girly way, that's not really me, and it's certainly not Jaz. But if you had to pick a word to describe the noise we were making, the word would be *squeal*.

Even as we were still making faces, my hands were on my laptop, and this time I didn't stop until I hit Return.

KTCoX: I like real music. Not yr soppy plastic gunk

My eyes were dancing, while my head filled with this buzzing sound, and...no, it was my phone. My phone was buzzing.

"Lacey?" I felt a little kick of unhappiness. "Aren't you *busy* tonight?"

"What are you doing?"

"Just hanging out with Jaz. Doing a little messaging. You know."

"Leave Kurt *alone*."

An hour ago she was too wrapped up with Paige and co. to talk to me. Now, though, now she was interested.

"Gosh, Lacey," I said. "Poor Kurt. I bet he's crying into his Karamel pillowcase."

"He's a sensitive, kind, real person, Katie."

"No, he's not. He's a famous person. They are not sensitive or kind. Everyone knows that famous people are selfish and annoying."

"You're pretty famous," said Lacey.

"What's that supposed to mean?"

A thump followed by a flurry of giggles. "Paige! I am trying to talk to Katie. This is important! Stop it. Stop it!"

Were they having a pillow fight? Life in the Savannah gang seemed to be one long tampon commercial.

"Come on, Lace," I said. "He's not a person like, say"—I tried to think of a person—"um…Dominic Preston. And I couldn't care less about his pathetic fans."

"Katie, you are…" Lacey searched around for the word, and I heard another thump, and then she hung up.

While I'd been wasting time with the new Savannah Mini Me, Kurt had come back for more.

> Kurt_Karamel: My music means a lot to me. I write from the ♥

My fingers raced across the keys, trying to keep up with my brain.

> KTCoX: U write to make money7. From girls who don't know better

"Too bad about the seven," said Jaz.

Kurt_Karamel: Coming from the new Justin Bieber

"*What?* I am not! Bieber is… I am *not a Bieber*."

"You did get famous by recording a video in your bedroom that then went viral and…" began Jaz, before seeing my face. "No. Of course you're not."

KTCoX: At least Im not a manufactured band who plays music writne in confrence rooms by middle aged men unlike SOMONE.
Kurt_Karamel: I don't need to defend my music to you.
KTCoX: Like you can call it music. U are the enemy of good music.

I hit return, then realized I hadn't finished.

People like u are—

Only, Jaz's hand was on top of mine. "Can we stop a minute?"

"What? Why? I was just getting going."

"Yeah. I think you need to calm down," said Jaz.

"I am perfectly calm, thank you very much." I mean,

I was breathing a little heavily, and one of my legs had started twitching all on its own, but let's be clear, I was in full control of the situation. "He's an idiot!"

"Yes. But"—Jaz studied my duvet cover—"it's a bad idea to do this kind of thing when you're worked up. Hey, let's go through your sister's stuff instead." Then, next thing I knew, she'd closed the laptop and was opening up Amanda's top drawer and lining up its contents on the bed.

"Um, I don't know if that's a good idea," I said, trying to drag my head out of the sharp, shiny world inside my screen and into real life again. "Mands is a total neat freak. She'll kill me if she thinks I messed up her stuff."

"And that affects me how?" said Jaz. "Where's the booze?"

"Amanda doesn't have any booze," I told her as Jaz dropped a load of socks down on the floor, where they were immediately sucked into the swamp. "She's even less exciting than I am. You should probably put those back."

"Okay, I'm over this now," said Jaz, who didn't seem in any hurry to put anything away. "Should I see if Nicole's around? She's been saying she wants to get her belly button pierced."

"It's too late," I said. "No place will be open."

"Pierced by me," said Jaz. "You can watch, if you want. Take photos."

"No thank you, Jaz," I said, opening up my laptop. My

life was complicated enough without Nicole's belly button bleeding all over it. "I want to get back to Kurt."

"Nah," said Jaz, nudging it shut. "You've done enough. Leave it now."

"Seriously, I don't mind upsetting him. He deserves it. For crimes against the top one hundred."

And now my heart was thumping, *bang, bang, bang*… no, it was my bedroom door. My door was thumping. "*Katie. Katie. Katie.*"

"What?"

"I have to get up early for work tomorrow," my sister said. "So I would really like some sleep."

And even I could see that denying Amanda access to her bed would lead to the kind of conversation I could do without.

"Maybe we *should* stop for the night," I told Jaz. "Thanks, though."

"For what? I didn't do anything. That was all you."

"Well, thanks anyway."

I unlocked the door, and there was Amanda. I smiled at her, but her face was not smiling back. It was doing the very opposite of smiling, in fact.

"What the—"

We looked at the contents of her drawers, spread all over everything.

"You do not touch my stuff," said Amanda slowly, sounding sad and angry at the same time.

"I didn't mean—"

"See ya then," said Jaz, flitting past her, down the stairs, and out the front door.

"I thought we were doing okay, sharing," said Mands. "I trusted you. And now I find you going through my personal things, with *Jaz*, of all people…"

"Mands, it wasn't me. It was all her. She just started looking—there was nothing I could do."

Amanda was shoveling her stuff out of my reach. "Fine."

And I wanted to tell her what had just happened. I wanted, no, needed, to talk to her, to figure out whether any of this was okay. In fact—

"Katie, shut your laptop and go to sleep."

And in case I was still in any doubt about her feelings, she turned out the light.

My World

Life is better
In my phone
While it's on
I'm not alone

In my laptop
Feels more real
My fingers talk
Say what I feel

Won't turn it off
Don't think I can
It's part of life
It's who I am

It's brighter there
I'm better there
Words that float so pure and free
I can be who I want to be
In a sharp and shiny
Lit-up world
That made itself for me

My screen won't tell me
I'm too young
It reads my words
Hears what I've sung

Yeah, those strangers aren't my friends
Only care when my name trends
But there, the party never ends
Never ends

It's brighter there
We're better there
Words that float so pure and free
I can be who I want to be
In a sharp and shiny
Lit-up world
That made itself for me

Yeah, tonight has been bizarre
Taking down a real star
I guess maybe I've gone too far
Gone too far
But

It's brighter there

We're better there
Words that float so pure and free
I can be who I want to be
In a sharp and shiny
Lit-up world
That made itself for me

Chapter Twelve

KATIE."

Someone was calling me. Amanda! Thank goodness. We were going to have the conversation we should have had last night.

"Mands?" I croaked.

"Katie."

Amanda sounded different. Her voice was younger and higher. More like Lacey's.

"Katie."

My bleary eyes tried to focus through a crust of sleep and yesterday's makeup. Mands was looking weirdly like Lacey too.

"Katie."

Could it be possible that my sister had somehow morphed into my best friend?

"Wake up, *Katie*."

"Aaaaaaaaaaargh…Lace?!"

I sat up to find Lacey at the foot of my bed. She was fully dressed, and she was looking rather worried.

"Are you okay?"

"I think so. Give me a sec." I took a deep breath and glanced around the room.

Little specks of dust danced in the sunlight. Clothes on the floor. My guitar in the corner. Amanda's perfectly made bed. Everything was where it normally would be. Except the person currently standing opposite me.

"Why are you here? It's Saturday morning. Shouldn't you be"—I tried to think what a normal person might do on a Saturday morning—"asleep?"

"I got my brother to drive me over."

"Wuh?" I know I sounded dense, but it was still very early. Not even eleven o'clock.

Lacey opened a paper bag and thrust something sticky across the bed at me. An apple turnover. I ate a piece and then the whole thing and began to feel slightly more awake.

"Fanks, Lacey."

I will say this for my BF. She may be a little fickle when it comes to her choice of companions, but that girl knows how to brunch.

"No problem. Do you want another one? They were on three-for-two."

"Split it?"

"Okay."

We had a quiet chew.

"Where's your sister?" said Lacey, looking over at her smooth navy duvet cover. Amanda's drawers were closed, the closet shut. It was as though last night's Jaz rampage had never happened.

"Went to work, I guess," I said.

"How can you sleep through someone else getting up right next to you?"

Lacey, I should say, cannot sleep with even a little bit of noise in her bedroom. I know this because when I stay over, I can barely breathe without her complaining. That girl hears everything. Even the tiniest possible fart. Which I hardly noticed I did until she started to laugh.

"I'm great at not listening," I said. "It's my super skill. Just as well, given that we share the room."

"How's that going?"

"Not very well," I admitted. "Jaz was kind of irritating her last night. I'm finding that friendship a little...difficult."

"Then why did you invite her?" said Lacey.

"Because you were at Paige's," I said, and we both went quiet.

"Um, yeah," said Lacey. "I came over to say sorry about that. It was, well, Paige was saying we had to go over all the pictures from the concert, and I totally forgot about the dance party and…" She saw that her apology wasn't going down so well and trailed off. "And I know you're going through some stuff, and I'm so…sorry."

"S'okay," I mumbled. "Cool."

I pried a piece of apple turnover from the roof of my mouth, chewed, and thought about it. What, exactly, had I been so worked up about last night? In the Saturday morning sunshine, with a nice breeze coming in from across the fields and the washing machine grumbling away downstairs, it was hard to remember.

"Hey, no school today," I said, suddenly feeling incredibly happy. "So are you sticking around? I should probably work on some stuff for my showcase thing. It would be nice to have some help."

"Sure," said Lacey. Then she added, "Maybe take a shower first."

♪♫♫♪

A few minutes later, I staggered downstairs to find Adrian sitting at the kitchen table. He was kind of frowning at me. "Morning."

"Why aren't you at the shop?" Saturdays at Vox Vinyl are so busy that it takes both Adrian and Amanda to keep a handle on things.

"There's someone at the front door for you. A journalist."

"What? Why? Aren't you going to let them in?"

"I thought we should have a chat first, make a plan… Katie, come back! Katie…"

I opened the door, and there, in the front yard, was a small man with brown hair, talking into his phone. When he saw me, he hung up right away and gave me a smile so huge I swear I caught a glimpse of his molars.

"Hi!"

"Hi," I said. "Can I help you?"

"I'm Chris. Chris Murrell. From NTV News. Could I by any chance use your bathroom?"

"Of course you can," I said, showing him inside. "It's in there. You have to flush it three times before it works, but that's normal. Have a good…one."

"Thanks!"

I turned around to see Lacey and Adrian making huge, silent faces at me.

What? I mimed.

Their mouths were moving very fast.

Slow down.

Their mouths moved fractionally slower. The toilet flushed three times.

Their mouths moved extremely big and fast.

"Hi!" said Chris the journalist, coming out of the bathroom.

"Cup of tea, Chris?" said Adrian, managing to make those few words sound like he'd lost a battle.

"Love one," said Chris, coming in and sitting down at the table like he was a Cox-kitchen regular. "So, Katie, love, love, love the new single."

"Milk?" said Adrian from over by the kettle. "Sugar? And how did you get our address?"

"Milk, one sugar, thanks. Now what made you write that wonderful song?"

"Oh. You really like it?"

Chris's eyes were gleaming. I had never seen anyone so awake before noon. "I absolutely *adore* it. You have a real talent for singing what the rest of us are thinking. It's going to be a hit."

"Um." I hadn't really thought of whether it would do well or not. But now that I did… "Do you think so?"

"I know so," said Chris. "And how it came out, leaked on the Internet, and by Kurt from Karamel. Everyone's all over the backstory."

"You certainly are," said Lacey, helping herself to my secret stash of Cocoa Krispies.

"I've never liked them," I said. "Boy band? More like boy bland."

"Ha! Ha ha ha ha ha!" Chris smacked the table in appreciation, making the Cocoa Krispies rattle. "That's really clever!"

Finally.

"And this must be a big week for you, single out, first concert. How are you feeling?"

"Look, sorry, but no," said Adrian, sitting down between us. "We don't know who you are—"

"His name is Chris," I said helpfully.

"Or where you're from—"

"NTV News," said Chris.

"You just show up on our doorstep, no explanation, and start questioning Katie, and that's not acceptable. Here's your tea. Milk, one sugar."

"Great, thanks," said Chris. "Well, okay, I'm a journalist, as I said, and a huuuuge fan."

"Thanks!"

"I'm just really excited about the next chapter of the whole Katie Cox saga."

"How did you get our address?" said Adrian.

"And I thought I'd get a couple of quick comments ahead of what's going to be a major few days for you! So this whole Karamel thing. I know where you're coming from. You've set up this battle, haven't you? Real music versus manufactured pop! The whole industry is starting to take notice."

"No!"

"No," said Lacey.

"Yes! And that online spat, last night, it was *fantastic*."

"What online spat?" said Adrian.

"I was thinking I might go back and delete that," I said.

Chris slammed his cup onto the table. "Katie, you can't!"

"I can't?"

"You know that your single's out the same day as Karamel's? We're thinking this could be a lead story. Battle of the bands!"

"Katie isn't a band," said Lacey.

"*What online spat?*" said Adrian.

Chris was looking as excited as I'd ever seen a person. Certainly more excited than, say, my manager and my best friend, who were, respectively, drumming their meaty fingers on the table and letting my precious Cocoa Krispies turn to brown junk. If you're going to steal a person's Cocoa Krispies, at least bother to eat them.

"So what we're thinking is, we lead with your crusade to bring music back to its roots. No more team-written singles for manufactured bands. Get the industry back to homegrown, genuine talent. People with something to say. Never mind good looks and Auto-Tuned voices."

"Katie looks okay," said Lacey.

"That's not what he meant," I told her, although a tiny part of me thought that maybe it was.

"And so it's you in one corner and your amazing new

song, and in the other, Karamel, with their overproduced single and stadium tour and T-shirts that cost fifty dollars each—can you believe it?"

"Fifty dollars! Who spends that much on a T-shirt?"

Lacey coughed. Then, when I looked at her, she said, "Savannah might have bought me one. Early birthday present."

"But it wasn't your birthday. It was my birthday."

"Have mine, if you want one that much."

"I don't want one."

"Then why are we—"

"You're the one who—"

"Ahem," said Adrian.

We looked up to see that Chris was watching us. It occurred to me that I probably shouldn't have an argument with my bestie in front of a journalist. Even if I *was* right.

"So," said Chris, as though he saw this kind of thing every day, "we thought, we'll interview Kurt in the wings at your concert, you doing your thing in the background, and then you'll come to his, and we'll do the same. Show both interviews that night, talk about your singles, see who wins. It's just what we're looking for right now, all the right elements, youth, music, social media…"

"All right…I guess…"

He stood up. "So that's a yes? Fantastic!"

"*No*." Adrian rose to his feet like a kind of mountain, if a mountain can be wearing a Keane T-shirt and need a shave. "I don't know how you got our address. But the answer is no. All our press goes through Top Music, and I imagine they'll take a pretty dim view of this…this… media intrusion."

I have to say it was very impressive. Only Chris didn't flinch. If anything, his smile got even brighter.

"Of course. Totally get that. But you know, it was Tony who gave me your address. Tony Topper? He loves the story. Even moved the single release dates around so that they'd coincide. He's one hundred and fifty percent behind it."

"You can't be more than one hundred percent anything," said Lacey, which was ironic because I was pretty sure she was 150 percent against this.

"Katie's too young to get into some power play to sell singles," said Adrian. "I don't think Tony Topper has her best interests at heart."

Chris's head jerked up. "Really? Can I quote you on that?"

"No!"

"Now, look," said Chris. "Maybe he doesn't. And I know that you do. I respect that. Which is why, I say, let's listen to Katie. Ask her what she wants."

"I…I…" Adrian was clearly trying not to say that he didn't care what I wanted.

"She's found her voice," said Chris. "Are we the ones to silence her?"

"Someone should," murmured Lacey.

Thanks, Team Katie. Thanks a bunch. In fact…

"Okay," I said, first softly, then loudly. "Okay! I stand by what I said last night. Let's do it."

"Terrific," said Chris. "I'll be in touch."

"I'm calling Tony," said Adrian.

Then we were back in the hall, and Chris was giving me a tiny salute, already on his phone as he stepped down into the front yard.

"She's a yes. Family's not interested, but…" And then he was gone.

There was one of those silences where everyone is shouting stuff in their heads.

"What?" I said. "Come on. Spit it out."

Adrian eyeballed me for a second. Then he said, "I can't argue with you on this one, Katie. I don't like manufactured bands any more than you do. And I agree, the industry's overcommercialized."

"But…?" I said.

"But…this is a big deal. You're going out there, saying this stuff. A lot of people will get upset. And when people get upset, they get angry. And you're so young. You have your whole life to tell the world what you think. I just figure that maybe, this time, you should keep your thoughts to yourself."

"So you're saying that because I'm young, my opinions don't count?"

"No, I'm not saying that."

"Because that's what it sounds like." Then… "Dad would let me."

I did know that this was the equivalent of pressing the big red button, and there'd be all kinds of fallout. And I wasn't happy about it. I wasn't happy at all, especially when I saw Adrian's face.

But—NTV News! I mean, *come on*!

"I can't stop you," said Adrian.

I looked over to Lacey, who shrugged.

"Great," I said. And then I said, "It's probably not that much of a story anyway."

Chapter Thirteen

ADRIAN WENT TO THE SHOP. Mom was at work, and Dad, who'd been out on a run, came in, took a long shower, and then settled down on the sofa.

So Lace and I stayed up in my room and tried to work out a set list for the concert.

Which was, now that I allowed myself to think about it, in four days.

Four days was really soon.

Breathe, breathe, breathe.

"I'll start with 'London Yeah,'" I said. "Because I'll be in London. That works, doesn't it? Or maybe I should do 'Just Me.'"

"Are you sure you don't want Savannah to dress you?" said Lacey. "She has these wonderful sparkly hot pants from her sister, and they're way too big for her, gigantic, really, so we thought…"

"I'm sure."

"Then what are you going to wear?"

"I don't know," I said, in a way that was supposed to indicate the subject was closed.

"FYI, Savannah's really good at dressing people. Look at me! I look great today. And that's all Savannah. I didn't even have to buy anything new. She's a genius with accessories."

The annoying thing was that Lacey did look great. She had this striped blue-and-white sweater she always wears, but instead of shoving it over jeans, she'd put it over a sleeveless blouse and miniskirt, and wrapped a skinny belt around it, which really showed off her waist and legs.

"Your belt is new," I said.

"Sofie lent it to me. Those three have the most gorgeous stuff, really. You should see it. Paige has a walk-in closet."

"So I'll start with 'London Yeah.' Then 'Cake Boyfriend.' Um, I might do 'Spaghetti Hoops'—I know Tony's not happy with that one, but I should do some new material. Then 'Autocorrect,' 'That Belt,' maybe the new one about my dad, 'Just Me,' and finish with 'Can't Stand the Boy Band.'"

"That was easy," said Lacey as her phone started to ring. "Oh, hi, Sav. I'm with Katie. She seems fine. She doesn't want you to dress her. I know. I know! I tried my best." She held the phone away from her face. "Sav says at least don't wear your jeggings."

"But I like my jeggings!"

She rolled her eyes and went back to her phone. "Yes. No. No, we can't. I know, but a sample sale at Cindy's is not as important as Katie's concert. Yes, you are coming too." I opened my mouth to say that if Savannah would rather go to a Cindy's sample sale she should go right ahead, but Lacey was still talking.

"What if she has a meltdown midsong? Or falls off the stage or something? This could be a complete disaster. Total public humiliation! You know what she's like. She needs her friends." She hung up and smiled at me. "Okay, I got Savannah to come."

"How generous."

Was I supposed to be grateful for this sprinkling of Savannah stardust? Just a few weeks ago, before the whole bedroom-recording-viral-music thing had happened, the Queen of Highlights, Princess of the Mani-Pedi, and High Priestess of Juicy Couture had not counted Lacey and myself among her loyal subjects.

More importantly, neither of us had even cared. Today, though…

"Katie?"

Dad was calling me from the sofa.

"What?"

"Come down! Now!"

Dad is not one of life's hurriers. This is a man who thinks that missing trains is not only normal but inevitable.

By which I mean, if he says, "Come now," you come. "What?" I hurtled into the living room. I forgot that the door was falling off and pushed it too hard. It fell off.

> "Katie Cox, with her new single 'Can't Stand the Boy Band' is unrepentant. The young singer-songwriter..."

"That's you!"

"That's me! And that's the man from this morning. He was in the kitchen, like, two hours ago."

"And he's talking about you!"

"Shh!" said Lacey.

> "...said on social media last night that Karamel are the enemy of good music, accusing them of playing songs written in boardrooms by middle-aged men."

"You tell 'em, Katie!" said Dad.

"Shhh!" said Lacey.

"Karamel have hit back, releasing a statement saying that they either write or cowrite all their songs themselves, and that they have the utmost respect for their fans. Head of Top Music, Tony Topper, spoke to NTV this morning, saying that both acts are releasing singles on the same day."

"That's him," I said. "That's Tony." He was standing there in an expensive-looking simple white T-shirt showing just a curl or two of chest hair at the neck, looking as relaxed as if he was watching TV, not on it.

"Shhh!" said Lacey.

"All I can say is that I respect them both. They're making great music. But the question for viewers is—are you Team Katie or Team Karamel?"

The screen cut back to Chris, smiling into the camera.

"The UK's most established act is up against one of its most exciting newcomers. It's the biggest chart battle in years, and so far, at least, this result is too close to call."

"That Tony's a genius," said Dad. "An absolute genius."

"He kind of is," I said. "I mean, I thought he was down on me because I wouldn't play one of his trashy songs. I assumed he'd given up on me. But this is…I mean, this is huge!"

"Yeah," said Lacey.

"So how's that set list coming along?" Dad grinned. "All eyes are going to be on you, my girl."

All eyes? "Uh, it's okay."

"Not feeling too nervous, I hope?"

"No…"

"Great! This is such an opportunity." He beamed. "My little princess, all grown up, out there, in the spotlight…"

"The thing is," I said, because his words were making my stomach do worrying things, "it's actually a very intimate concert. Low-key. Tony and I agreed that we'd start small."

"Doesn't look small from where I'm sitting," said Dad.

"Very small," I said, mainly to myself. "Small and intimate and low-key."

♪♫♩♫

I turned down Savannah's offer of that pink limo to take me to the gig, and in the end, it was Adrian who drove us there, four sleepless nights later, to a soundtrack of the Pet Shop Boys and early Pulp.

It wasn't the most fun of journeys. I was playing songs over and over in my head, until none of them made sense anymore and I completely forgot why I'd written them. Meanwhile Adrian was mainly swearing, at the traffic, at other drivers, and at the lack of decent road signs on the highway. So much so that I hardly registered when he started banging his fist against the steering wheel.

"Ach."

"What is it?" said Amanda.

"See for yourself," said Adrian.

The road outside the venue had been blocked off by some kind of humungous demonstration. A hundred or maybe two hundred people were standing around doing protest things like holding hands and chanting and waving homemade signs.

"Why are they doing it here?" I said. "They have all of London to stand around and shout."

"I hadn't heard anyone was marching today," said Mom.

"This isn't an ordinary demonstration," said Adrian. "They're too young."

Now that he mentioned it, they were all around my age or younger, wearing T-shirts and hoodies and little tiny skirts, with fluffed-up hair and angry faces.

"They're—" Adrian paused. "Ah. I wondered if this might happen."

It was then that I read the closest sign. It said:

> ## KATIE COX IS A WITCH

Which made me read the other signs. I got:

> ## KARAMEL FOREVER

> ## BAD APPLE

> ## KATIE HATER

> ## UGLY FACE UGLY SOUL

And then I decided I would stop reading the signs.

"I'm sorry. What's going on?" asked Mom, who really needed to get with the program.

"They're Karamel fans," said Amanda. "And I think they're kind of mad at Katie."

"I am not a hater," I said. "I just happen to be giving my opinion about something, which is that I hate it."

"Speaking of which," said Adrian, "K, maybe you want to turn away from the window?"

Given the view, this was not a difficult decision to make.

"Yeah. Let's make it into the venue alive," said Amanda, which I think we all felt was unnecessary.

Thank the Lord I hadn't gone for the Savannah limo. Adrian's car was old and dented and smelled of cigarettes and mints, but it was, at least, reasonably anonymous.

Too bad I couldn't stay in it forever.

"All right?" A man with an earpiece was talking to Adrian through the window. "Around the back. Don't worry. It's ticket holders only."

So Adrian attempted a three-point turn, which quickly became a twenty-seven-point turn, while I tried to tune out the chanting.

And then Mom said, "Why do you always have to upset people, Katie?"

"I'm just saying my opinion."

"Yes, but you're famous now. Your opinions matter."

"And they didn't before?!"

Mom's fingers began to massage the area between her nose and her forehead.

Then I was safely housed in a dressing room with "Katie Cox" taped to the door. Only it wasn't safe, not safe at all, because in half an hour I would be onstage performing in front of two hundred and fifty people.

My brain took in the office chairs, the bunch of flowers with a note from Top Music, the two bottles of mineral water, one fizzy and one still, anything to distract me from the fact that in half an hour I would be onstage performing for two hundred and fifty people.

"I can't believe that in just half an hour you'll be onstage performing to two hundred and fifty people!" said Lacey, who *had* traveled in the Savannah mobile.

"That's so many people," said Paige.

"And you haven't even done your makeup," said Savannah.

"Yes, I have," I said.

"Oh," said Savannah.

With eleven of us in the room, plus my guitar, it was starting to feel a little claustrophobic.

"Can I get you anything?" said Adrian.

"A drink would be great," said Dad.

"And for me," said Jaz. I have no idea how she got there.

"I meant Katie," said Adrian.

"I'm fine, thanks," I said.

The walls, which were a very deep green, seemed to be closing in on me, like I was being suffocated by spinach. I shut my eyes.

"Katie." Amanda's voice sounded far away. "Are you okay?"

"Fine," I said, opening my eyes to see Lacey looking down at the scrawled piece of paper that was my set list.

"You're going to play 'Can't Stand the Boy Band'?"

"Yes," I said.

"Even though you know how much it upset all those Karamel fans?"

"Um…" I said, because she was maybe a little bit right. I mean, I'd known that my song would annoy people, but not so much that they felt like they had to make signs and come to my gig to protest…

This was a bad idea.

Not just the song, not just the chart battle, but this concert.

Everything. All of it.

Dad was strumming on my guitar, while Savannah was demonstrating to Paige the perfect way to use lip liner, using Sofie's mouth as a canvas. I sank down into a chair and put my head between my knees.

Then, Adrian's voice: "Okay, that's it. Everyone out."

"What?"

"You don't mean me," said Savannah.

"I do," said Adrian. "I'm Katie's manager, and I want this room clear in the next thirty seconds. Go find a place to watch. Or get a drink. I don't care. But *go*." He caught my shoulder as I headed for the door. "Not you, bozo."

"Oh." I looked back at the room, which was now wonderfully empty. "Hey, thank you."

"I'll call you when it's time," said Adrian.

Ten minutes to go.

I tuned my guitar and then retuned it. I sang a few notes into the mirror, which had lights all the way around it, and reapplied my eyeliner.

Five minutes to go.

Don't be sick. Don't be sick.

Then I went into the bathroom and threw up.

There was a gentle knock on the door. "Katie?"

"Yeah."

"You're on."

Chapter Fourteen

THERE WAS A THICK DARKNESS to the wings. Deep and thick and I was in the middle, down deep, in the depths of my very own grave.

I could hear them, the audience, the two hundred and fifty people who were about to see me completely fall apart.

Someone tapped me on the shoulder. "Katie, hi!"

"Yaaaaaaargh!"

I must have jumped about ten feet into the air. "Sorry, Katie, it's Chris. From NTV News. You remember?"

"Oh, right. Hi Chris." I'm not the world's greatest conversationalist at the best of times, and this definitely wasn't the best of times.

"You remember the deal? We're just going to have a quick chat with Kurt while you're singing. He'll be here in a minute. If we can get it edited in time, we're looking at a slot on tomorrow's ten o'clock news. Have a great show!"

And before I had time to think or even breathe, the lights started doing some crazy whizzing around, and this huge voice came down from the sky or maybe the speakers, and Chris stopped muttering because I knew I was going to have to sing.

"Ladies and gentlemen…"

I don't want to be here.

"She's a rising star. Our youngest, freshest, realest talent…"

Please, let me be somewhere else.

"Give a very warm welcome to…"

Anywhere else.

"*Katie Cox!*"

I hesitated. And then, on legs that felt like they were someone else's, stepped out from the darkness into bright, bright light.

It was like when you do a somersault in the swimming pool and halfway through forget which way is up. For a long second, I couldn't see anything, couldn't hear anything, and then, slowly, the world settled.

They were there, just beyond the end of the stage. A blur, face melting into face, shifting, coughing. I could smell their hot breath.

Through the murmuring, a single, lonely *whoop*.

"Um," I said, sliding into place on a chair and trying to tilt the microphone so it was closer to my mouth. It wouldn't move. I tried harder.

It wouldn't budge and wouldn't budge, and I was seriously considering giving it a whack with my guitar when it occurred to me I could just move the chair up. So I did that.

"Hi."

The front row began to focus. Lacey next to Amanda. Jaz. Nicole. Savannah, Paige, and Sofie. Tony. Mom. Dad.

They seemed…excited. And then, less excited.

The more I stared into the audience, the more they shuffled and looked away. As though until two minutes ago they had really been worked up about seeing me in the flesh. But now that I was here, my flesh pale and sweaty and trembling, everyone was starting to think it might have been better to have stayed home.

I know I was.

"So I'm Katie Cox. Like the apple. Cox apples. Not that there's an apple called Katie, but maybe there should be! Ha ha."

I swear I heard Jaz sigh.

"So, yes. Katie Cox. That's me."

I glanced sideways. The darkness was only three steps away. Two steps, if I made them big ones. I could be off the stage and out the back door in, what, a minute, maybe a minute and a half?

In fact, I was just wondering exactly how much money I'd owe Tony if I ran out now when I noticed that I was somehow still talking.

Isn't it amazing what the human body can do?

"So. Anyway. I'm going to p-play you a couple of songs. More than a couple. Some songs. Of mine. That I wrote."

With the most enormous effort that anyone has ever made, I managed to lift up my guitar and get my numb fingers into position on the strings.

"This one's called 'London Yeah.' Because we're in London. Um, yeah. Yeah! Yeah."

I strummed the opening chords.

> Trafalgar Square and then Big Ben
> Bond Street and Covent Garden
> Greenwich and the Cutty Sark
> And a really massively big Primark
>
> Put your hands in the air
> For London, yeah

This was okay. I sounded a little wavery, but it wasn't too bad.

> Camden Town and Kensington
> Notting Hill and...

And...where?

I'd forgotten the next line.

In a fraction of a zillionth of a millisecond, I raced to the part of my brain where I kept all my lyrics and...

Nothing. Completely empty.

Like a cathedral if someone had taken all the seats and altar out and switched the lights off. And maybe, right in the middle, left a tiny piece of paper that said "Sorry."

> Camden Town and Kensington
> Notting Hill and...Aberdeen

Where had I gotten *that* from? Aberdeen *isn't* in London. Not even slightly.

But it did rhyme. And is, at least, a place.

> Greenwich and the Cutty Sark
> And a really massively big Primark

> Put your hands in the air
> For London, yeah

No one put their hands in the air, either for London or for me. I got to the end of the song, and there was an embarrassed pause, then a dribble of applause.

Just the whole rest of the concert to go.

"Okay, cool, thanks. This next one is called 'Cake Boyfriend.' I wrote it because my friend Savannah… She's here, in the front row. Hey, Savannah"—Savannah quietly pulled her jacket over her head—"she had this gigantic cake at her party, and she loved it so much it was almost like a boyfriend, and I thought, Wouldn't it be great to have a cake that was a boyfriend? Anyway."

> Pat-a-cake
> Pat-a-cake
> Baker's man
> Bake me a boy as fast as you can
>
> Give him fudge for hair
> And frosted blue eyes
> And finish him off with

Twanggggg.

I'd snapped a string.

"What is wrong with me?"

Adrian appeared at my side and took the guitar as I stood, now shaking, and the audience began to whisper and rustle.

And I thought, *I won't even have nightmares anymore. Not now. There won't be any point.*

Adrian handed me back my guitar, and I strummed again. Out of tune.

Now the murmurs were getting restless. In fact, some of them had stopped being murmurs and become real conversations. Probably about me being completely terrible.

Words floated up in front of my eyes, words from those signs, just outside.

KATIE COX IS A WITCH.

BAD APPLE.

UGLY FACE UGLY SOUL.

They were right, of course. I was useless and ugly and wrong. The people outside knew it. Everyone inside knew it too. I should get off the stage now, crawl back under my rock, and stay there forever.

"This is going really badly, isn't it?" I said, more to myself than anyone else.

There was this *huge* laugh. And I began to play.

Pat-a-cake
Pat-a-cake

Baker's man
Bake me a boy as fast as you can

This time, it was better. I even started to feel it, a little, toward the end, so as it finished I played straight through the applause, on into "Autocorrect," then "That Belt."

That belt
That belt
That turquoise belt
With sparkly stones and pieces of felt

From the back, people were joining in.

Six ninety-nine
And it could have been mine
With sparkly stones and pieces of felt

My fingers were behaving. My voice seemed to know what to do. The singing from the audience got louder, and I could hear Adrian, Mom, and Dad.

I was…I was almost starting to enjoy it.

My dad rocks hard
My dad is ace

My dad plays lead guitar
And drums and sax and bass
My dad's way cool
My dad's so fine
My dad lives his dreams
And shows me mine

Now the audience wasn't this frightening thing anymore. It was more like a wave or a huge blob of power, and I was riding it or feeding from it or something, because the more it cheered and stamped, the better I felt. Especially when I went into "Just Me," and everyone held up their phones and swayed.

Then it was done and…

"So this is the last song," I said. "I know it's been a little, erm, controversial. But hey. It's something I really believe."

I picked out the first few notes.

Can't stand the boy band…

And—I'm not kidding—the room went *crazy*.

They knew all the words, every last one, and they half sang them, half shouted them along with me.

Plastic faces, stupid hair
Can't stand the boy band

The matching clothes they wear

While most of me was there, in the room, a small part of me was saying to Tony, *See? We're not stupid. We are not sappy idiots, ready to be fed your mushy pop.*

The tattooed Chinese symbols
On the skin that's perma-tanned
I can't stand the boy band

Louder.

Don't like the boy band
Singing songs about their grans
Don't like the boy band
Hanging around their camper vans

Their lyrics are predictable
Their music's oh so bland
I don't like the boy band

I want to be *here*, I thought.

Oh, poor sweet boy band
Your music makes me heave

Exactly here, exactly now.

You poor sad boy band
Soon one of you will leave

Forever.

And if you think you'll be remembered
Then you misunderstand
RIP the boy band

I couldn't stop. They wouldn't stop. We roared it again and again and again.

Can't stand the boy band
Can't stand the boy band
Can't stand the boy band

And as they chanted, I pulled the microphone up, and it came away from the stand so easily, and I shouted, "This is for real music! No more manufactured garbage! No more overproduced tracks! No more Auto-Tuning! No! More! Boy bands!"

A spotlight swung across the audience, and as the beam swept through, I saw that everyone was cheering. Except…

the light caught a face. Lacey. She was watching me with eyes that burned.

"No more boy bands," I said. And then, finally, I let my guitar drop.

"Thanks very much. Good night!"

Chapter Fifteen

WITH ONE LEAP, I WAS in the wings. Wings?! It was like I *had* wings. It's such a huge cliché, but really, I was bouncing, floating, a sort of human hoverboard, surfing high on the applause, hugging my guitar to me, feeling like Christmas morning and the end of exams and glittering swimming pools under summer skies, only a million, billion times better.

"That was awesome!"

"Oh my God, thanks!" I panted at the darkened face, which smiled and moved out into the light and became…Kurt.

Kurt from Karamel.

If I'd been a hoverboard, I would have run out of batteries. As it was, I sort of went, "Uhhhh."

He was younger than I'd thought. No, that wasn't it. I hadn't really thought of him being any age, because in my head, he didn't have an age, because of not being a real person.

Now, though, I saw that he wasn't much older than me and not hugely taller, either. He was much better-looking than me, though, like his eyes and nose and mouth were all fighting to be the best thing on his face. Of course, it didn't help that *my* eyes were still funny from the spotlights, so one second, I was looking at his nose, and then it turned into this swimmy burst of yellow and then back into a nose.

"I'm not saying I loved the last number. But the rest was great. I can't believe that's only the second time you've played live. I was puking from nerves for at least my first twenty gigs."

"Actually," I said, my voice far steadier than my legs, which were wobbling all over the place, "I did puke. Before I went on. You can't smell it, can you?"

"No."

"Phew."

We stood there, listening to the cheers turn to claps to the sound of people picking up their jackets and stuff, and I tried to process the fact that I'd just led two hundred and fifty people in an anthem against Kurt from Karamel and then asked him whether or not I smelled like vomit.

"So, look," said Kurt, "I have to go. My car's here. But see you tomorrow night, okay?"

I stared at him, feeling as stupid as I've ever felt, which, let me tell you, is really very stupid. "What's happening tomorrow night?"

"Your turn," said Chris, who was also still there, as it turned out. "We interviewed Kurt when you were doing all your 'I hate boy bands' business. Such a great visual. And then we'll do your interview while he's singing his single. Tomorrow night at the O2."

"Okay, yes. Um, see you tomorrow. And—oh, Tony! Hi!"

Tony Topper had his hand on my elbow, guiding me toward a different door, leaving Chris and Kurt to melt into the darkness. "Come on through. Come on through."

"To where?" I was still holding my guitar.

"Your party," said Tony. "Nothing big, just a few people from Top Music, some press, the guest list…"

We went through a heavy door, straight past a woman with a clipboard and into a room that was completely full of people.

And—ooh. I put my guitar down. Because there was a waiter with a tray. Of things.

"Can I?" My stomach was feeling very empty.

"Sure." Then Tony saw that I'd taken three chicken satay sticks. "Although we really must have that chat about a personal trainer."

"*Ka-aa-t-iee!*" Paige came exploding in like she'd been fired from a cannon. "You were *am-aaa-zing*!"

"You were pretty good," said Savannah, just behind her. "Except at the beginning, which was lousy, babes. You need to work on that."

"Um, thanks," I said.

"And—" Savannah stopped and wrinkled her nose. "Can you smell puke? I can smell puke."

Then, thank goodness, Mands and Mom were racing across the room.

"You were awesome!"

"So amazing."

I glowed. I actually glowed.

"Although"—Mom had her hand on my arm—"the song about your father…"

"I'll write one about you too," I said. "For the album. It's only fair."

"That's not what I…" She sighed. "And…I just…do you have to be so *angry*, Katie?" She looked out across the party. "Everyone was so angry."

"It's just a genuine expression of my dislike of the way the music industry is going," I told her. "What used to be real has become a corporate machine designed to manipulate young people, and I want to bring things back to the music. Enough greed…" I trailed off. "Are those *tiny quiches*?"

Mom didn't look especially convinced. "You

sounded great, but all this rage, it's not you. And if you say things like that, you're giving the other side a reason to hate you."

"Then let them," I said. "I can handle it."

She pulled me into a sudden hug. "But you're still my little girl."

"*I am not.*" I decided to focus on the important part of the conversation, which was that I'd sounded good. If Mom couldn't handle my impending adulthood, that was her problem.

Sofie was taking selfies with pretty much everything in the room. Savannah was messaging frantically, while Nicole and Jaz were throwing miniature samosas off the balcony. And Lacey…

"Hey, BF," I said to the lone figure lurking by the coats.

"Oh." Lacey looked up and attempted a smile. "Hey! Good job."

"Thanks. Did you have fun?"

"Yeah. Thanks for inviting me. I mean, I still don't like that last song. And the one about your dad was a little much. But the rest was great."

"Okay, well, we can agree to disagree, right?"

"I guess," she said. "Ooh, are those mini pizzas?"

"Pesto flatbreads," I told her. "Go get 'em, girlfriend."

I stood and watched, feeling weirdly outside of

everything, seeing as how it was supposed to be for me. Flat. Flat as a pesto flatbread.

"Oy! Princess! Over here!" Dad's arm wove around my back. "You rocked my world tonight."

"I did?"

"So hard. You are a great talent, my girl."

"I am?"

"Those lyrics! That tune!" He swiped up my guitar and began to strum 'My Dad.' "Phenomenal," he said.

The people closest to us were beginning to turn around, and for a second, I started to feel embarrassed. Only then, as Dad's fingers rippled up and down the strings, and everyone started to smile and tap their feet, I remembered.

This was Dad.

And when Dad plays, it's like your ears are filling with sunshine.

A circle was forming around him, so I moved back and out of the way.

"Well now." It was Tony. "It seems you have tapped into something, Katie. I'm not often proved wrong. But this time…"

"So I'm forgiven?"

"Make the top ten, and you're completely forgiven." He laughed.

"When does it go on sale?"

"Midnight tonight. And…you're sure? You don't want any production on it whatsoever? Because we can ramp up the bass, smooth over the vocals. No one ever needs to know."

"Absolutely not," I said. "I mean, that's the whole point, isn't it? I want the sound raw. Unmixed. Real. True."

"True," repeated Tony. "Maybe that can be the name of your album?"

"Yes!" I said. "I like that. *Katie Cox: True*. You're really good at this!"

"I know," said Tony.

Dad looked up from his guitar and gave us a wink.

"I got a few emails from him," said Tony. "More than a few."

"Oh, yes," I said. "He wanted to send you his demo."

"And he did," said Tony. "Several versions." We listened for maybe twenty seconds, as Dad slid from "Hotel California" into a jazz version of "Sweet Child o' Mine."

"The surprise is he's good."

I had this moment of relief, which turned into a thud of guilt. What had I been expecting? Dad was a professional. Too much time around Amanda, that's what it was. "Of course he's good!"

"Have you heard of Papaya?" said Tony. "She's fresh from kids TV, making her first album. I could put him on it."

"Could you? That would be fantastic," I said. "I know he's looking for work right now. When would he start?"

"Recording's in a few weeks' time. Nice little studio in West Hollywood. I'll get the contract over…"

Dad was beaming as his hands danced an impossible dance across the frets, and I remembered the feeling of seeing him on the doorstep, the smell of him, how he'd held me, tight, against his jacket. And how far away Hollywood was. How very far away.

The party seemed to freeze, as though we were in a movie or something, and in my head, I walked over and looked Dad in the eyes and tried to say good-bye again. Had an actual, honest attempt at sending him back to California and Catriona Version 2, whoever she might be. Soon I'd stop remembering exactly how his face moved, let alone the way he'd grab me for a sudden hug, or…

"I'm not sure it's a good idea, actually," I said. "Dad's had a few problems."

Not what Tony was expecting. "What kind of problems?"

"Oh, you know," I said lightly. "Personality problems. It's kind of well known that he's a little…unreliable. You'll expect him in the studio, and instead he's on a plane to the other side of the world, without even—" I caught myself. Where did *that* come from?

"I'm glad you told me," said Tony. "Papaya's a busy girl. She can't wait around for some no-show guitarist."

"Better that you know now," I said, snatching another satay stick from a passing waiter as Tony drifted away.

The waiter didn't move, though, so I took another stick and then another, swallowing hard down a throat that had gone painful and dry.

Anything to keep Dad here. Anything.

Chapter Sixteen

IT'S GOOD TO KNOW WHAT your strengths are. My particular strengths, in no particular order, are:

- pizza (eating, not making)
- music (making, not eating)
- sleep

The morning after the concert, I was really focusing on that last one. In fact, I woke up only when a pair of underwear hit me in the face.

"Murhph?" I removed them and opened my eyes. "Ugh! Mands, your underwear went in my mouth!"

"Calm down," said Mands. "They're clean."

I sat up to see that every inch of the room was covered in her clothes. And her phone was blasting out Alanis Morissette.

Seriously. When it comes to sleeping through things, I'm the best.

"Rise and shine, superstar."

"Isn't it Thursday? Why aren't you at work?"

"Day off," said Amanda. "I'm doing my spring cleaning." Alanis finished, and her phone started playing something by a very famous band that I am not allowed to name.

"Hey, Dad's playing on this."

"*Is* he? I thought they did all their own guitar work."

"So did Dad. Apparently not."

We stopped and listened for a while. Now that she'd told me, it was completely obvious Dad was playing. The notes were sliding up and up, more like a voice than an instrument. Dad can make a guitar sing.

"It's been funny, having him back again," said Mands, holding a navy top up against her chest. "There's lots of stuff I forgot that he did."

"Like what?" I asked.

"Like that dee-dah tune he hums in the shower. The same one, every morning."

"Oh, yeah!"

"And"—Amanda tossed the top into a pile and reached for a floppy sweater—"that jangly thing he does with his pockets. Or how his socks never match. I wonder what else I'll forget?"

"Why would you forget anything else? He's not going anywhere."

"Not now, but"—she set the sweater on the bed,

smoothing down the arms as though it were a frightened animal—"you know he can't stay forever, don't you?"

"I don't see why not," I said. "I don't mind giving up the den. We never go in there."

"It's not good for Mom and Adrian," said Amanda. "And…it's not good for us."

"Speak for yourself!"

Amanda did that thing she does where she goes from being this cool friend-type person who happens to look a lot like I do to becoming a kind of cross between a headmistress and a queen.

"Katie. Listen to me because I know you. And I get that you and Dad are close. But the way you are when he's around, that song you did last night, it's like you're in love or something."

"You're saying you don't love Dad?!"

"Of course I'm not saying that. All right, not in love, but you go all starry-eyed, and it's like you can't see when he behaves in a way that is completely unreasonable."

"Like how?"

"Um, okay. So, for example, Mom and Ade are pretty hard up financially right now, but Dad has not offered them a penny."

"He's broke. He spent everything he had renting the dolphin apartment and—"

"Exactly! He squandered his cash away renting something completely unsuitable, and now he's back and he's broke! You have to tell him to go home, Katie. He listens to you."

"This is home." I got up and headed for the door. There's only so much a girl can take before breakfast.

"It's your home. It's not his home."

I was almost out of there, but I paused in the doorway, just long enough to say, "It's our home. And he's our dad."

♪ ♫ ♫

Me, Lacey, and Mad Jaz had parked ourselves on our special area of grass at school. Lace had her legs stretched out in front of her, attempting to get a little bit of a tan. Jaz was sitting in the shade. Sometimes I think Jaz carries the shadows around with her, the way other people might have a big handbag or BO.

"What was your favorite thing about last night?" said Lacey. "If you had to choose one thing."

"The part where I snapped Amanda's bra strap," said Jaz.

"You snapped Amanda's bra?" Amanda-Jaz relations were bad enough already. "What? Are you nine or something?"

"Yeah," said Jaz, looking very pleased with herself.

"I liked it when you got into the music and stopped

shaking," said Lacey. "Until then, I was worried you were going to puke."

"That took a while," I agreed, feeling my phone buzz in my pocket.

A text.

> Can't wait for the interview tonight. Car will pick you up at 5:30 and take you straight to the concert. Ten o'clock news, here we come! Chris

Oh, yes. That. The Karamel concert. It might be nice to bring some moral support. Even if the support thought I was without morals.

I glanced over to Lace and opened my mouth. Only Jaz spoke first.

"So when's it out?"

"The single? It's out now."

"I might get it later," said Jaz.

Now, Jaz isn't one of the world's greatest shoppers. By which I mean, she's great at choosing stuff, but she seems to have kind of a block on the paying part of the process. So the idea of her turning over actual cash was really very exciting.

"If you buy it on CD, then I'll sign it," I said. "Vox Vinyl has a lot. What about you, Lace?"

"Join the dark side," said Jaz.

"So," said Lacey, in what was the most obvious change of subject in the whole history of changing subjects. "Are you going to ask Dominic Preston out?"

"Why would I do that?"

"Because of being in love with him."

"I am not in love with him," I said, making our private gesture for shutting up at her, because my love life (or lack of it) wasn't something I wanted to go into very much around the unpredictability that was Jaz.

"You said you really liked him," said Lacey. "And he seems to like you, and the dance is next week. So ask him out!"

"Only if you ask someone out too."

"Like who?"

"Um…Devi Lester?" I suggested.

"Katie, I don't have to go out with someone just because you are. We are different people."

"But I'm not going out with anyone," I said, trying to picture asking Dominic Preston out and finding it very, very easy to imagine him saying a big fat no. "I'm…I'm too busy with my music right now. You know. Writing my album. Also, it's not like I need a man to give my life meaning." It occurred to me that it would be good if Lace had a boyfriend. If nothing else, it would take the heat off me. "But you should totally get together with Devi."

"So *I* should go out with someone because my life is so

very empty and meaningless," said Lacey. "Thanks, Katie." Which was not what I meant at all, and she knew it.

And I knew she knew it. And she knew that I knew she knew it.

"I'd better go," I said. "Need to get my stuff figured out so I can make a quick getaway after school."

"Why?"

"Because," I said, as pointedly as I could, "I have to go all the way to the O2 for a Karamel concert, just to do a stupid, annoying interview. Total waste of an evening. Later."

♪ ♫ ♪

"Katie, there's a big silver car outside. Apparently it's for you."

Mom did not sound impressed.

"Oh, that," I said, peering out the window. "Yes, that's for me."

Which is when I remembered that I hadn't especially told her about the whole news-at-ten shebang.

"You do not have my permission to go out unaccompanied on a school night. And—"

"*Hey! Katie!*" It was Dad, waving both arms.

I headed for the front door, Mom just behind me.

Dad was standing in the driveway, next to a confused-looking man in a suit.

"Sorry, what's going on?"

"I'm supposed to be driving a Katie Cox to the O2," said suit man.

"Oh, are you?" said Mom.

"Er…yes…?"

"Katie, we seem to be having some fairly serious communication issues. You were out last night. Fine, okay, that was a special occasion. But there is no need for you to go gallivanting off again this evening."

I wasn't totally sure what *gallivanting* meant, but I could tell it wasn't good.

"It's a press thing," I said, trying to sound as reasonable and mature as I could. "For the single."

"In what way is going to the O2 related to your single?"

"Well, I'm going to be interviewed while Karamel are singing, and I'm going to say how I think they are destroying music. It's going to be on the ten o'clock news!" Mom was getting less impressed by the second. And she hadn't been impressed to start with.

"If you had told me in advance, I might have said yes. But you didn't. So the answer is no."

The man in the suit looked awkward. "Can't take you without parental permission," he said.

"That's all right. I'm her dad. Of course she's going!"

"Benjamin…"

"Er, Dad..."

"What?" Dad was practically dancing on the spot. "He's chauffeuring you to a concert! Take a tip from your old dad, Katie—never turn down a freebie."

"Katie is in deep water, Benjamin. You saw what it was like last night. She needs to take a step back and—"

"Last night was a huge success!" said Dad.

"Last night was terrifying," said Mom.

He put his hand on her arm, and I saw her try not to flinch. "Zoe, love, you're not a creative person. You can't be expected to understand. But I'm like Katie. I get it. I'm with her on this. And I'll look after her."

Mom was looking distinctly unhappy. "I don't want her going off into the middle of goodness knows where all on her own..."

Now, I have to say, in the interests of family harmony, I was beginning to think that I might give up. Some things are worth fighting for, but a Karamel concert isn't exactly one of them. Plus, despite my epic sleep, I was sort of feeling kind of tired. I figure even Beyoncé couldn't deal with a concert followed by a whole day of school. An early night and a happy mother—it was an appealing combination.

"Then I'll go with her," said Dad. "It would be nice to have some time for just the two of us."

"Really? Because—"

"Come on, Katie," he said, looking up from inside the car, where he'd already sat down and—wow—even taken off his shoes.

I ducked my head, but Mom still managed to catch my eye and held it, steady and unhappy, and there was that pulling sensation I hated so much, more than anything.

Would it never go away, that feeling I'd had for years and years, every time they argued, and in those still, cold hours after the shouting had finished and Dad was "taking a nap" or Mom was just "going for a drive" where I was stretching in two directions at once, tighter and tighter and tighter, and I knew if I made even the smallest movement I would tear apart—would it never let me be?

"You coming, princess?"

A whole evening with Dad, though.

"I'll see you later," I told Mom, climbing in beside him. Her mouth opened wide, but then we were off down the driveway, leaving her, and whatever it was that she was shouting, behind.

♪ ♫ ♪

"This is fun, isn't it?"

I looked up to see Dad pouring himself a glass of something from a mini fridge.

"Um, yeah."

"I could get used to this." He downed his drink and poured out another. "Want something?"

I lifted up what turned out to be a bottle of hard cider.

"I don't think so," said Dad, nudging it away. "Hey, someone has to be responsible here."

"I wasn't going to have any. I was just seeing what it was."

"Of course you were," said Dad, opening up a little bag of peanuts he'd got from somewhere. "How about one of these? They're wasabi flavored!"

I took one before remembering that wasabi is basically mustard, which is basically disgusting.

"Hey, that Tony's not the easiest guy to get hold of, is he?"

"Oh," I said, making sure to look out the window so he couldn't see my cheeks turning red, "Tony's very busy. But I'm sure he'll get back to you. Be patient."

"Of course, of course," said Dad. "And it's nice to have a bit of a vacation. Spend some time with my girls."

Just to get it done, so that Mands would let it drop and we could all get on with our lives, I took a deep breath and then another one and said, "Do you think it's okay for you to be staying so long?"

"Yeah, yeah," he said. "It's fine! I mean, I know your mother is a little uptight. And that Adrian, he's, well, he's not exactly... But they don't mind really. They would have said!"

"That's what I thought."

No, Katie, do it right.

"But, Amanda, she thinks it might be good for you to..." No, I couldn't tell him to move out. I just couldn't. In the last second, I switched the words: "Pay some rent."

"Ah, Miss Sensible," said Dad. "She'll go far."

I wasn't sure what to say to that.

"Thing is," said Dad, "I don't have much. Money."

"I thought you were extremely busy? That everyone wanted you?"

"I am," said Dad. "Just...not...currently."

"But don't you have a lot saved up?"

"Not...really."

This didn't seem quite right. Because the one thing we'd heard during the divorce and after the divorce and in the weeks leading up to the divorce was how Dad was, in Mom's words, "swimming off with half a house in his back pocket." Mom wouldn't lie. Of course she wouldn't. Only Dad wouldn't, either.

"I don't understand," I said slowly. "I thought...the settlement..."

"It was a great apartment," said Dad, and from the look on his face, part of him was still there. "Dolphins! From the kitchen window! And I was busy. Busy enough to justify it at the time…only, not quite busy enough. And Catriona needed money. For—"

"Her Pilates studio," I finished for him. Catriona's stupid Pilates. It had been bad enough when they were still together. Now, even after they'd split, it was still making my life a misery. "Dad, you have to ask for it back."

"That might be a little…"

"And then you can pay Mom some rent, and everyone will be happy."

"I'm not…"

I leaned my head on his shoulder, like I used to when I was tiny. "And then everything will be okay, and you can stay for as long as you want. You can do it, Dad!"

I couldn't see his face, but I felt his voice through his chest and down my ears and into my heart. "For you, my princess, I'll give it a try."

We sat, like that, for maybe a couple of minutes, the car going down the highway so fast that it felt like we were flying—and I was perfectly, completely content.

Chapter Seventeen

EVERYONE AT THE O2 SEEMED to know who I was without me having to tell them. I was swept down hallways, passed from one person to another like a human relay baton, from offices to dressing rooms, then around a corner and into a tunnel, until I was standing in the hot darkness behind a curtain along the edge of the stage, with little flutters of something in my stomach.

Nerves? Well, that made no sense, since there was nothing to be nervous about.

Probably just leftover angst from yesterday, I told myself, feeling the heat of the many, many, *many* people out in the crowd. I couldn't see them, but then, I didn't have to. I could hear them singing and chanting and feel their happiness, their excitement, and their sheer energy. And as much as I wanted to find it pathetic, there was something a tiny bit infectious about all that joy. In fact—

"Katie, hi, hi."

"Hi, Chris." Beside me, Dad was looking expectant. "Dad, this is Chris. He's a journalist. He's going to put me on the ten o'clock news."

"Chris, hi—Benjamin Cox." Dad gave him his best smile, the one that's like floodlights.

"Hello, Benjamin."

There was an awful lot of helloing and shaking of hands. Then, finally, Chris said, "So, we thought we'd interview you during 'Clap Your Hands,' the boys' new single. It's toward the end. Stay here and we'll set up, and then when the song begins, I'll start talking."

"So I have to sit through a whole entire Karamel concert?" A guilty part of me thought how much Lacey would have loved it. In fact, I was wondering if I should call her so she could listen in and trying to figure out whether I had enough minutes left to cover the whole thing when—"You came!"

"Kurt. Hi. Um, yes, I came."

He was standing *right next to me*. "I didn't think you would!"

"Well, I did," I said.

And Dad said, "Benjamin Cox, musician. If you ever need someone…"

"Pleased to meet you, Mr. Cox," said Kurt, looking for all the world as though he was pleased to meet my dad.

He was dressed completely stupidly, in this billowy shirt thing, over a pair of neat, sharp jeans. And his hair—it was sticking up in about thirty-seven thousand tufts, all pointing in different directions, like a kind of human mop.

"Have my card," said Dad.

"Thanks," said Kurt, sticking it into his back pocket. "Hey, sorry, but I have to go. The opening act finished a long time ago, and the crowd's getting restless. See you after?"

"I don't know. It's a school night. I have homework."

"What?" said Dad. "Of course we'll stick around."

"Cool," said Kurt. "See you, then."

I was just breathing a sigh of relief that he was leaving when he turned and shot me an awkward grin. "Enjoy the show."

"I really won't," I said to his departing back.

Now, the noise from the audience had gone from loud to supersonic, and around me, people with headsets and radios and things were running about, doing whatever it is that they do, which seemed mainly to be trying to change one of the light bulbs in a ten-foot-high letter K.

"This is great, isn't it?" said Dad. "Ringside seats for your favorite band."

"Where did you get that from?" I asked him. "Karamel is not my favorite band. Not even close."

"Really?" Dad sounded surprised.

"Did you, um, didn't you, notice, that the new song, didn't you notice what it was, you know, um, about?"

"The one about me? Which was terrific, by the way. Might see if I can get Taylor to cover it."

"No, the one about boy bands. Dad, you do know why we're here, don't you?"

Dad opened his mouth to reply. But then…the lights blazed.

The crowd roared.

And Karamel bounded onto the stage like a basket of upturned puppies.

"*Hello, O2!* Are we feeling it?"

"No," I murmured.

Kolin and Kristian were clapping, and—of course—it was absolutely perfect that Kurt had a microphone *and* the lead guitar.

I sighed. "That guitar is beautiful."

"It's a Gibson Les Paul," said Dad. "Very nice."

"Wasted on him."

Dad said something, but I never heard what, because as he began to speak, they began to play, and a wall of sound crashed against the crowd, making them scream and flash and fling their hands into the air.

Like puppets, I thought, just as I noticed that my left foot was tapping to the beat.

"I said, *are we feeling it?*"

Kurt's supple fingers were gliding across his guitar. Exactly the sort of fingers that those idiotic girls were probably imagining brushing across their backs or running through their hair.

"Then let's go!"

Ugh, his confidence was revolting. He should have shown at least a little bit of shame, if he had any self-respect whatsoever.

"We are so excited to be here tonight! We're gonna start with something new…"

Streaks of yellow fire shot up from the front of the stage as they began to sing, and there was no doubt about it, Kurt really could sing—and it was sort of uplifting:

Wings beat faster in my heart
Kiss my lips before we part

I found myself leaning in. Then leaning out, because, come on.

And then leaning back in again.

Hurts inside, but now I see
I must let the bird fly free

I rubbed my finger across my wrist. Goose bumps.

Let the bird fly free

The darkness around me seemed to dissolve, and now I was in a new place, where fireflies flitted above and droplets of dew shimmered in the summer light and… No, my ears were wrong. This was Karamel. It was hopeless and awful and…

Little bird, so free

And then there was the way the chorus lifted and lingered, before collapsing into a glitter of notes that seemed to rain down over my head and…

Fly home, bird
To me

The final note held, then broke, and then, before I could even catch my breath: "Now for our first ever number one. Get ready…for an all night part-aaaay!"

I tried to imagine I was somewhere else, listening to something halfway good, not this terrible garbage that was making me sway and then pulling me onto my very tiptoes.

In fact, if I really concentrated, I could forget about Karamel altogether. Forget about the way that their music came at me like a sky full of doves, swooping and soaring, racing across fields, skimming the sea before hurtling up, up into the blue...

No, not birds, something rich and lovely, a chocolate cake with a million layers...

Forget the way Kurt's fingers slid across his guitar like it was a part of him, like he was running fast downhill with the wind behind him...

Oh my God.

"Sing with me, O2!"

My hands were in the air, and my vision began to cloud with bursts of gold. The lights maybe, or it could have been the chords themselves, bursting out of the air, filling my eyes with the same fire that flowed from Kurt's fingers.

"Are you okay?" shouted Dad. "Katie, you're shaking. Katie? Katie?"

"Help me," I murmured, but my words were lost in the wonderful, awful, wonderful music.

Chapter Eighteen

MINUTES, OR MAYBE HOURS LATER, there was a tap on my shoulder.

"Katie, are you ready to go?"

"Whu…?"

"Great!"

I just had time to realize the person talking was Chris, and there was a TV camera pointing right into my face, when…

"So, Katie, tell me, what is it that you so dislike about Karamel?"

A few meters away, Kurt was bent over the microphone, eyes half closed.

"I, um, I don't like their music."

"Yes, but why?"

"Because…" Wow, how had he just jumped to this topic? *How?* "It's very…I don't…it's not…very…good."

"Twenty thousand people out there seem to disagree."

"Yes. But. Yes."

Chris gave me a funny look, then turned to talk into the lens. "While Katie Cox never actually names the subject of her new single 'Can't Stand the Boy Band,' clearly, Karamel, the world's number one boy band, must be who you're talking about?"

"Um, maybe."

"You've been extremely vocal in your dislike of manufactured bands, of Auto-Tuning, even their expensive merchandise came in for criticism. As you said when we first spoke, who has fifty dollars to spend on a T-shirt?"

"The T-shirts? Oh yeah. They're exploiting their fans," I said, wondering vaguely whether Dad would lend me fifty dollars.

"So to conclude, Katie, why should viewers buy your single and not theirs?"

Something about his rather snarky tone pulled me out of my daze, and I managed to look into the camera and say, "Because they are fake, and I am the real deal. I'm Katie Cox, and my music is true. That's why."

"With the two singles now out and battling for the top spot on the charts, only time will tell. Handing back to the studio now for the news."

♪♫♪

The craziest thing is that I can't even remember the end of their set. I must have been sick or something. Certainly my head was sort of burning, although in another way I think I experienced every single moment more vividly than anything that had ever happened to me before.

The last notes died away, and the three of them ran from the stage.

Dad was looking around. "Come on. Let's go find this party, okay?"

"I don't know," I said. And I didn't. I didn't know anything about anything.

"You need something to eat," said Dad. "They always have food at these things."

He led me down some steps, me stumbling like I had just gotten over the flu, and then through an open door, and I could hear music and laughter, and I stood, my head resting against the wall, my eyes half closed, trying to make some kind of sense of what was happening to me...

"Well? Still think we're plastic?"

I opened my eyes, and there he was.

"Yes, actually," I said. "You totally had a wind machine. That part where you all walked forward, with your shirts flapping around? That is *exactly* what I was talking about."

"Ha! Yeah, all right. But—"

"And you all sat on barstools. Er, cliché much?"

"They were not barstools! They were…just…high stools that we…all right, they were barstools."

"And that video, the one they projected while you did the song about the party. With you all jumping around. You were in a camper van. And then you all walked off into the sea at the end!"

He was really laughing now. "You know why we had our backs to the camera? It was so cold when we were filming that Kristian was crying."

"Really? Ha!"

"Anyway. Thanks for coming. I'm sorry you didn't like it. I've never played like that before. I wanted you to… I'm just sorry that I couldn't convince you that we're not what you think we are."

I could sort of feel my heart hammering in my chest, the blood pulsing in the very tips of my fingers, as I said, "There were a few moments that I didn't completely hate."

He looked up. "Wow. The praise is too much for me to take."

"I liked that riff you did on the beginning of the one about your mom."

"Huh. I was trying to be the Edge."

"Well, you weren't. But it still sounded good. And that first song, the bird one, was…kind of…amazing." There was a silence. My breathing felt far too loud. To cover it up, I said, "Plus, you have an okay voice."

"Just okay?" He laughed that lovely laugh. "Katie, admit it. I saw you cheering."

"I was not."

"You started out just standing there. By 'Big Love,' you were jumping up and down. And at the end there, I could see you singing along."

"Stalker!" I had to stop myself from the thrilling idea that even while he had all of the O2 to sing to, he'd noticed me.

"Should've brought you onstage."

"In front of that many people? I don't understand how you can do it."

"I wasn't confident to begin with," said Kurt, like he was telling me this great secret. Maybe he was. He was talking fast, his cheeks all flushed. "But…I love being onstage, making music. It's the only time I ever feel like I'm really being me."

"I feel that too," I mumbled. "Like, I can't say stuff well at all, I'm totally failing English, and half the time I can't even have an actual conversation. Lacey—she's my best friend—she thinks I have verbal dyslexia, which I don't think is a thing, but if it is, I absolutely have it. Only, when I'm singing…"

"You're being your true self," said Kurt.

"Yes."

I had to make a conscious effort to remember that I didn't like him.

"It's funny," Kurt was saying. "I saw your video of 'Just Me,' and it was like, like a bomb going off in my head. I thought—I understand her. I get where she's coming from. That sound, pure, spontaneous—we need to get back to that."

"Really?"

"Yeah," said Kurt. "And then, when I heard 'Can't Stand the Boy Band'…it hurt."

My phone was buzzing in my pocket. Mom. Many, many missed calls. "Look, I have to get home. Where's my dad?"

We looked across the room to see him laughing in the middle of a big group of people.

"Your dad's pretty fun. I loved that song you did about him."

"Thanks," I said. "Everyone else hated it."

"It's nice that you're close. Mine left when I was seven. Came back when the band got big, of course." He dropped his eyes. "Anyway. Doesn't matter."

"I'm lucky," I said.

"You are."

There was this moment.

"About this stupid chart battle…" he began.

"Oh. That."

"May the best man—"

"Or woman," I said quickly.

"May the best man or woman win."

Then he turned and went into his party.

"So to conclude, Katie, why should viewers buy your single and not theirs?"

"Because they are fake, and I am the real deal. I'm Katie Cox, and my music is true. That's why."

"With the two singles now out and battling for the top spot in the charts, only time will tell."

I LOOKED UP FROM PAIGE's IPAD and across our classroom to see Savannah's top lip curl in a way that, on anyone else, would not have been pretty. Since it was on Savannah, it was still very pretty.

"Babes, what happened?"

"Were you nervous?" asked Paige.

"Um, I guess so."

"Because that was"—Savannah searched for a word, then not finding one, went with two—"car crashy."

"It wasn't that bad," said Lacey.

"My boyfriend Kolin is seriously upset about it all," said Savannah. "I mean, he's totally rising above it because that's what he's like, but he is upset."

"I'm sorry I upset Kolin," I murmured.

"I think Kolin can take care of himself," said Lacey.

"But you were so weird," said Sofie. "It's like you forgot how to speak or something."

"Like she was sick. Or crazy. Like she was having a breakdown!"

And I was starting to think that maybe I was when Lacey spoke up.

"Come on, Katie. Let's go."

We went down the main stairs, past the drama bulletin board, which was crowded with drama types all looking at some drama thing, and then the sports bulletin board, crowded by sports types all looking at some sports thing.

"Sorry about Savannah," said Lacey.

"Hey, that's okay," I said. "It's not like you're in charge of her."

Lacey scrunched up her face. A face that, I noticed, was lightly coated in some kind of moisturizer that made her look sort of damp.

"What?" said Lacey, her hand going to her cheek.

"Just, your skin…?"

"Oh. Yeah. It's supposed to be 'dewy.'"

"You want your face to look like wet grass?"

"I did when Sofie got us all sample bottles. Is it awful?"

"No. Just a little shiny."

She smushed it around with her palms, leaving two patches of pink. "Better?"

"Kind of. But, Lace, don't let me stop you from looking dewy."

"I won't," said Lacey, slowing down to give the vending machine a longing stare. "I'm stopping myself. Anyway, if I wanted to buy a jar, it'd cost a fortune. So it was never going to be a long-term thing."

I wanted to ask her whether she actually liked hanging out with Savannah and co., but maybe that was my answer. Reaching into my pocket, I found some change and popped it in. "Whaddya want?"

"Ooh. Kit Kat?"

There's always a worry with vending machines that the candy will get stuck, and then I'll shake the thing to try to get it out, and the whole thing will tip over and crush me to death, which apparently happens more often than you'd think. I once said this to Amanda, who replied that I worry too much, and told me that people get killed by everything, from bee stings to their own bedsheets, which gave me even more to worry about. Luckily, on this occasion at least, the Kit Kat came tumbling straight down into the bottom.

"Here." I offered Lacey half, and she took it. "Um, you know…in the interview…on the TV last night…was I really that bad?"

"You were fan-freaking-tastic," said Lacey. Which meant that yes, I was.

"I wish you'd been at the concert with me," I said, and I did wish it too. "You keep me sane."

"I wish I'd been there. You watched Karamel from the side of the stage. What a waste."

"Lacey," I began, "what I told you. About…them. Karamel. I think maybe I said some stuff I didn't mean. Well, that I did mean, at the time, but now…"

Lacey was now into her second stick of Kit Kat, peeling away the last few flecks of silver foil. "Katie, it's okay. I understand."

"You do? Thank goodness! So here's the thing. I'd heard them before, of course I had. But I'd never *heard* them until last night. And—"

"And now you're lying about how you feel about Karamel so you can be my friend again." I was about to set her straight, when she went on. "Which is really nice of you and everything. But I don't want you to tell me that you like them."

"You don't?"

"You're you, Katie, and you hate Karamel. You don't like their music or their fashion or their high production values or even that they're popular. You hate the mainstream. And that's not something we agree on, honestly, but it's who you are, and you are my friend, and your life is difficult enough right now without me abandoning you too."

"Um."

"Friends forever!" said Lacey.

"Er, yes."

"It's like you said. You're real, and you're true. And sometimes we're going to disagree. But you need to be able to be yourself. Or what's the point of us being friends?"

"Mmm."

She took a bite, then grinned at me, a tiny blob of chocolate on her front tooth. "So what was the worst thing about last night? The most annoying thing they did? You're going to tell me anyway, so I might as well ask and get it out the way."

I was feeling extremely uncomfortable, and not only because Amanda had shrunk the skirt I was wearing in the washing machine.

"I don't know that I could pick a specific moment.

There was a chord sequence that went into this song about a sunset beach. It was actually technically incredibly accomplished…and also very, very bad. In a technically accomplished way."

Lacey threw a handful of wrapper in the trash. "What else? Go on. You know you want to."

"Er. Okay. I didn't like the way Kurt—that's his name, right?—Kurt looked out into the audience like he was about to kiss them all. He did this thing with his eyes. And his hands. It made me feel weird." That, at least, was true.

"I know what you mean," said Lacey. "It does seem a little like they want all their fans to be in love with them so they can sell them music. And I dunno. I've been thinking. And I do love them. But—"

"Because I've been thinking too," I said quickly, "and I don't mind if you want to talk about them a little. Like, not a lot, because you're right—it's way boring. But if you, say, wanted to lend me a couple of their albums or something then we could play them and discuss them, maybe after school tomorrow if you want? Bring everything you have."

"I don't want to do that," said Lacey. "Because I know you wouldn't like it."

"I'm just saying, if you did, then I'd be totally up for it. As a favor to you. Tomorrow. Or tonight. Or the day after tomorrow if you'd like. Whenever, basically."

"Katie, it's fine."

"No," I said. "It's not. I know you're pretending you don't care about them as much as you did, but secretly deep down, I think that you do. And so I am willing to put my, er…prejudices aside, for one night only, or a few nights, and do a complete Karamelathon, completely immerse myself in their work, in order to save our friendship."

"That's very generous of you, Katie. But honestly, our friendship doesn't need saving."

"Doesn't it? Because, I dunno, recently, I've been getting the feeling that—"

I stopped because Lacey wasn't looking at me. She was looking at her phone.

And I did think, if this girl is about to tell me we are BFFs while simultaneously texting Savannah, then I will…

"Look, K."

She held it out. There, in her iTunes library, was "Can't Stand the Boy Band." Artist, Katie Cox.

"I bought it."

"But you already have it. I sent it to you. Way back. That's how all this started."

"Yeah, but, Katie, this is a chart battle. And if there's going to be a battle, of course I'm fighting for you."

"Oh, Lace."

Sensing that I was about to do something incredibly

embarrassing like cry in the hallway, she brought out a pair of headphones. "Want to?"

We looped them in one ear each and sat on the dining hall steps, very close.

Can't stand the boy band

"It's you!" Lacey squeezed my hand. "Your new single."

"Yes."

"You were so worried, and now, here it is. I'm proud of you, BF."

"Thank you," I said in my smallest voice. We listened as well as we could over the noise of a bunch of sixth graders walking by. Even with that, and with the fact that I could hear it through only my right ear, I caught a scratch in my voice as I went into:

On the skin that's perma-tanned

Plus, the guitar seemed thin, all on its own, without even a bass line to shore it up. My brain reminded me of the lushness that was Karamel, and I found myself saying: "You don't think it sounds kind of, er, underproduced?"

"To me it does," said Lacey. "But then, we know I like my music overproduced. So I don't think my opinion counts."

"It does!" For the second time in ten minutes, I found myself wanting to cry. "Your opinion totally counts!"

"It doesn't," insisted Lacey, "because I don't know about music like you do."

"Maybe I don't know about music. Maybe I've been mouthing off about something without taking the trouble to really understand it."

She smiled. "You wouldn't do that."

"Lacey," I said, because I was genuinely worried that my head might explode or fall off or something, "I have to go."

"Now?"

"Yes."

"But…we're listening."

"I know." I had to get away. "Sorry. But I have a bus to catch."

"Can't you get the next one?"

"No. I said I'd be home at six. It's the chart announcement."

"Good luck," said Lacey. "Not that you need it."

Death by
Vending Machine

You can die by duvet
Or pillowcase
You can die from a storm
If you're in the wrong place
You can die from bouncing off
a trampoline
Or being crushed by a candy vending
machine

You can die by wasp
You can die by bee
You can die from slipping
On a single pea
Or getting caught in the wheels of a
pink limousine
Or being crushed by a candy vending
machine

You can die onstage
Or in your room
You can die of guilt
You can die of gloom

You can die of regret for what might
have been
Or being crushed by a candy vending
machine

Chapter
Twenty

TWENTY MINUTES LATER, I WAS curled up on the front seat of the bus with my head resting on the window, its frame vibrating against my cheek. I had my lyric book out, but for some reason, the page kept filling up with curly *K*'s, plus the occasional *aramel*. All right, more than occasional.

"What are you writing?"

Jaz had strayed from her usual back-seat territory to come and peer over my shoulder.

"Just songs," I said, moving my palm to cover the page. Which, to any normal person, would have been a signal that my words were private and not to be looked at.

Unfortunately, while Jaz had clearly noticed part one of the signal, part two was not on the agenda. She shoved my hand out of the way and stared.

"Why do you keep writing the word *Karamel*?"

"That doesn't say Karamel," I said.

We both looked at the ink scribbles. It very obviously did say Karamel.

"Because I hate them so much."

Jaz didn't seem very satisfied with this explanation. "Are you secretly obsessing about Karamel?"

"Lay off, Jaz. I'm not secretly anything."

"Touchy."

"I am *not* being touchy!" It came out disturbingly high, like I'd sucked in helium. Which Amanda had done once, at my cousin Dean's wedding, and then freaked out about it and had a very squeaky panic attack. "I'm so not!"

Clearly sensing she was on to something, Jaz leaned in. "Ve-ery touchy."

Time to do some damage control. I straightened my features and pushed back my hair and cleared my throat. "Jaz. Listen. I know you like a little bit of scandal, and I get that you think you're onto something here. But, if you remember, I hate Karamel. Really hate them. I hate them so much that I wrote a song about exactly how much I hate them, which is a lot."

"Fair enough," said Jaz.

"Good. I'm glad we got that straightened out."

The bus rumbled along for a while, and I allowed myself to relax. The car behind us honked. And I was just feeling my cheeks get back to a normal kind of temperature when:

"I'm just saying," said Jaz. "If there's anything you want to get off your chest…"

"There isn't!" I said.

"Because if there is…?"

"There is not."

"Are you sure?" said Jaz.

"I am sure."

"Really sure?"

And then, I knew it was crazy, and I knew I shouldn't, but I had to tell someone…because it was too difficult to keep it all secret, like I was a glass, and someone was pouring water into me, more and more and more until I was overflowing. Jaz had probably figured it out by now anyway with her weirdo psychic Jaz skills. Plus, saying it out loud just felt right.

"And they began to play, and I realized I'd heard them lots of times, but I'd never really heard them. And then I did, and it was amazing! Like nothing I've ever felt before, Jaz. It was mind-blowing. My mind was blown. Is blown! It was like…like religion or something! They are so incredibly talented! Like, a zillion times more than anyone else in the world who's ever lived! The stuff they can do…the sound they make…and Kurt, he's kind, and he's funny, and he's so, so sweet. You know, he didn't have to forgive me for hating on him. It really upset him. But he did because he's a decent person. And as far as the rest of the world is concerned I can't stand Karamel, when in fact I can't seem to stop obsessing about them. Oh, Jaz, what am I going to do?"

"Yeah, I was not expecting that," said Jaz.

♪ ♫ ♪

When I got home, Dad was in the kitchen, digging through a pile of takeout menus.

"Katie, what would you like for dinner tonight?"

"Er. It's just, we're kind of waiting for the big announcement. About the whole chart thing. So I'm a little…"

"Food's on me! Anything you're craving?"

I was feeling more sick than hungry, so I just said, "Chinese please. Actual takeout, not from the store."

"Done! Where's your mother?"

"Here," said Mom, taking off her jacket. "I've just got a text from Ade. He's stuck in traffic. He'll be back in a sec, and…will you please get off me, Benjamin?"

"Zoe, don't say I never spend money on you!" He had his hand on her waist. "What would you like, my princess? Anything at all."

Mom's eyes said she'd like for Dad to go away, but she said, "Chinese takeout is fine."

"Chinese takeout it is!" He spun her in a little circle.

Or at least he tried to. Mom wasn't really having it, so he got her halfway around, and then she bumped into the oven. "Sorry, Zo."

A big sigh.

"And look," he said. "This is…important. It's meant a lot, you giving me a place to stay. Really, it has."

Mom mumbled something that might have been, "S'okay."

"And I know we're family, and you'd always do it for me…"

Another sigh.

"But still. I appreciate it, my darling. Now will you take this and go buy yourself something nice?"

And—whoa—he handed her this *huge* wad of cash.

Mom was as shocked as I was. So shocked, in fact, that at first she didn't say anything but just made fish faces. Then, finally, she said, "Benj. This is…too much."

He dipped his head. "I owe you."

"Well, yes, you probably do, in fact. You definitely do. But this, this is"—she thumbed through it—"thousands."

"A couple of thousand. Don't spend it all at once! Or do! Take yourself into town. Dress up nice for a change. Speaking of which…" He leaned down behind the table and lifted up this enormous cardboard box. "Here, Katie. For you."

"Right." Then, as I clocked what was written on the

box—which was the word *Gibson*, I said, "Seriously? Like, *seriously*?"

"Open it!" said Dad, with that expression I recognized from Christmas morning.

I tore into the box. And there, nestled down under a ton of packing material…was quite literally the most beautiful guitar I'd ever seen.

"Oh my God, Dad. Oh my God."

"You like?"

I threw my arms around him. "I love it. And I love you."

"I have something for your sister too." He hesitated, then took a little box out of his pocket. A little box in Tiffany blue. Wow. He really had gone shopping. "Do you think you could give it to her for me?"

"Of course," I said, and then, when Mom headed to the bathroom, I caught his arm. "Hey, I'm so glad you talked to Catriona."

"I…uh…no problem. Anything for my little superstar."

"I'm not a superstar yet."

"You're going to be number one," said Dad. "I just know it."

"I'd be happy with top twenty," I said.

"Number one," said Dad. "Come on, Katie. Dare to dream! And let's get this Chinese ordered, okay? Always takes longer than they say, and I'm starving."

I'd just opened the menu and was trying to decide whether Dad's newfound generosity would stretch to beef in black-bean sauce *and* chicken-and-shrimp chow mein when the front door slammed in that heavy way that meant it was—

"Ade," said Mom.

"Haveyouheardanynewspleasetellme," I blurted out.

"Let the man take off his jacket," said Mom.

Which I did, and it took about a hundred years.

"They beat me, didn't they? Tell me that it was close at least."

"Chillax," said Adrian, despite some very specific instructions from me never to use that word. "It's not out yet. Tony's going to text me. But, look, whatever happens now, I want you to know how proud I am. How proud we all are."

"Yes, yes," I said. Then, because that sounded a bit ungrateful, I added, "And thank you. For supporting me. I know I've made things difficult recently. And, you know, not only recently. But anyway. Thank you."

"You've been standing up for what you believe," said Adrian. "Of course it's difficult. But it's worth doing." He glanced at the clock. "Any minute now."

Mom took my hand.

Dad took my other hand.

Ding!

Adrian picked up the phone, his forehead creasing.

"Well? *Well?* Tell me! Actually, don't tell me. I can't stand it. No, do tell me. Tell me!"

"Katie," said Adrian. "Karamel's single debuted at number two."

"*And?*"

"And yours is at number seventy-eight."

Chapter Twenty-One

IT'S FINE," I SAID. "IT's exactly what I was expecting. It's completely fine."

Three concerned faces stared across the table at me, like a group of sad owls.

"I mean, come on!" I told them. "They're a hugely successful boy band with gazillions of fans. I'm just me. There was no way I was ever going to even come close to winning this."

Mom went to squeeze my shoulder, and then she saw my face and thought better of it.

"You don't need to feel sorry for me."

"Love," said Mom. "This industry, I don't want to see you hurt…"

"I'm not hurt," I said. "I am annoyed. But I always knew this would happen. Can we please not talk about it anymore?"

"Well…" Mom began.

"I mean it," I said. After all, how could she even begin to understand? She didn't get it. She couldn't get it. Not her and not Adrian. In fact, there was only one person who could.

"Dad. I—"

He looked away. "I'll go pick up that Chinese? Won't be gone long, it's, what, ten minutes' walk? Not paying the delivery charge if I don't have to."

"Okay. But maybe don't get anything for me. Turns out I'm not hungry."

I walked very slowly up to my room.

Then I sat down at my desk and burst into tears.

♪ ♫ ♪

There's a reason that people in movies generally cry while facedown on a bed or sliding down the back of a door.

You don't see them crying onto a desk, and that's because, as I quickly discovered, crying directly onto a desk is incredibly uncomfortable. Plus, when I finally sat up, I found that I'd been leaning on a red felt-tip pen, and it looked like my cheek had been burned.

The best music had won.

I'd known it when Lace and I had listened to my song on the steps. Heck, I'd known it the second Kurt had opened his mouth at the Karamel concert.

What should I do now?

What *could* I do now?

I could tell the world that I'd changed my mind. No, not changed my mind. That when I'd written "Can't Stand the Boy Band" I hadn't known what I was talking about.

That was Old Katie. New Katie had seen Karamel play. She was converted. New Katie loved Karamel.

Then, I'd shake their hands, if they'd let me, and...

Ding!

Just heard. Coming over

Lacey. My best, best, best friend. She'd stick with me. She'd understand that everyone makes mistakes.

Ding!

Just heard am coming over

So loyal that she'd sent the same text twice!

Plus, it would be good to come clean with Lace. Once she'd forgiven me, it would make our friendship even stronger.

That's the thing about me and Lace. We've had our ups and downs, for sure, and the downs have been really bad. But it's what makes the rest of the time together so great. Like, for example, when we had that monster argument over who copied whose Julius Caesar essay. Now that we're over it, we're better friends than ever. Even though, come to think of it, she never did admit that she'd stolen her introduction from me, and to be honest, it's still a tiny bit annoying.

Bang, bang, bang!

Lacey was thumping on the front door. I scampered down the stairs and opened it, arms wide for a full-on hug, and:

"Hi," said Jaz.

"What? What are you doing here?"

"I texted," said Jaz.

"No," I told her. "*Lacey* texted. Lacey is on her way over."

"Hi," said Lacey, coming up the driveway. "What? Why so surprised? Didn't you get my message? And what's *she* doing here?"

"Supporting Katie," said Jaz.

"*I'm* supporting Katie," said Lacey. "Ugh! What happened to your cheek? Is that a burn?!"

Unscheduled gatherings are normally a complete no-no. I thought Mom would probably cut me some slack, given current events, but I still made sure to get everyone upstairs and into my bedroom as quickly as possible.

"It's just disgusting," said Lacey as I closed the door behind her. "They can't be content with winning. They have to crush you. How dare they? How actually dare they?"

"It's not their fault," I said. "They have a huge fan base, and they're really g… Some people think they are really good."

"You should have won," said Lacey.

"Nah," I said.

"You're so real and true, and they're just this manufactured…"

"It is a little unfair," I said. "I mean, talk about David and Goliath."

"Are David and Goliath in Karamel?" said Jaz. "I thought they all began with a *K*."

"You know nothing," said Lacey.

Jaz didn't flinch. "I know more than you think," she said.

Lacey gave her a superior smile. "Hey, look, Jaz, it's great that you're here, but me and Katie, we're best friends, and we have some stuff we need to talk about."

Jaz picked up my liquid eyeliner and gazed down at the bottle. "Oh, so now you're here for her, are you?"

"Yes. I am."

"Now that you can pity her?"

This is why it's important to keep friends as separate as possible. Ideally on different continents. Mind you, the way Lacey was looking at Jaz at that moment, even continents wouldn't have been enough to stop World War III starting. Different planets?

"You are poison, you know that, Jaz?"

"Lacey…" I began.

"Fine," said Lacey. "But she is."

I have to say that Jaz wasn't at all bothered by Lacey's accusations. She just sat there, using my liquid eyeliner to give my Amy Winehouse poster a mustache.

"They just made an announcement," said Lacey, reading from her phone. "'*Peace and love to all our fans who bought the single and to all who bought Katie Cox's song. The music lives forever. Xo.*' That is rude!"

"Um, yeah. So rude."

Lacey lay back on my bed and twiddled her hair. "You know what? I think I'm starting to get why you're so annoyed by them."

This was it. The moment to come clean. "Lacey?"

"Yes?"

I must have said it in a fairly significant-sounding way because she sat up and let her hair drop.

The words were all ready, lined up in neat rows inside my mouth, like a little wordy army, poised to fight for the truth.

And they did come out. But not from me. "Katie has something to tell you," said Jaz.

"What?" I said.

"What?" said Lacey.

"I'm surprised she hasn't said it already. Given that you're 'best friends.'"

"I'm sure she did tell me," said Lacey. "Katie tells me everything."

"Did she tell you that she's in love with Karamel?" said Jaz.

"*What?*" said Lacey.

Which is when I knew I couldn't say it. Not here.

Not now.

"Of course I'm not in love with Karamel. Jaz, you are not making any sense. Where would you even get that from?"

Jaz's face hardened. And it was pretty hard already. "Cool. I'll just let you go on with it then."

"Go on with what?"

"Living your lie."

"I'm not living a lie."

"Go away, Jaz," said Lacey. "Get back to wherever it is you came from and leave me and my BFF alone."

Jaz's head swiveled from me to Lacey and back again, and she blinked a couple of times, but she didn't seem even slightly phased. That's the thing about Jaz. You can't hurt her. She's made of whatever they use to line saucepans.

"I'm leaving," she said.

"Good," said Lacey.

"No, stay," I said weakly. "Unless it's important. Or, you know, not important."

And then she was gone.

"Where does she get that garbage?" said Lacey.

"I know," I said, hating myself, and Jaz, and myself all over again.

"So?" said Lacey. "What are you going to say to them? You can't let them have the last word."

I opened my laptop and thought for a second. Lacey was watching the screen as I typed:

> To all the fans who bought my single, THANK YOU.
> Karamel—u guys still suck. And yr army of zombies
> doesn't change anything. Rock & roll K x

I hit return. "Okay. Done. It's all finished."

"Finished?" said Lacey, the color rising in her cheeks, like when Mom has that cocktail involving cranberry and orange juice. "This is just the beginning."

"Of what?" I said.

"Your comeback."

"Oh. Because I was kind of thinking I might shut up for a while."

The flush was now all the way to the top of Lacey's face. "It's not like *nobody* bought the single. You're at seventy-eight!"

"Which is garbage."

"It is not garbage. It's really good, and you are only

going to get better. You are going to build on your fan base, and you are going to write more great songs. I believe in you, Katie."

"That's great, Lace," I said. "But, honestly, I'm not sure that I do believe in myself."

There was a weird sound, like a cat meowing, and for a second, I thought maybe the mice had learned a new skill, only then I realized it was Lacey's phone.

"New ringtone," said Lacey, bouncing to her feet. "Sofie did it for me. Do you want it for yours?"

I shook my head.

"Mom's outside in the car," said Lacey. "Gotta go, K."

"Thanks for coming."

"I'm so glad I did," said Lacey. "Remember: you are—"

"Don't say it!"

"And you'll always be—"

"Please…"

"My number one," said Lacey.

"Ugh, you are so cheesy," I said. "Get out."

She got out.

I was on my own.

The bedroom felt incredibly empty. Like there were too many spaces between the molecules of air. Spaces that, under any normal circumstance, I would have filled with music.

Something like…I scrolled through my playlists…

Amy? Nah, too dark. Mraz? Too light.

What I needed was…no.

No…

Yes.

A quick few taps and there they were, three boys beaming from my screen, the notes flowing through my headphones and lifting me up and away from all the weirdness, onto a golden cloud where everything was still okay.

Lacey was completely right. It had all been pretty humiliating, but I'd come through just fine. Number seventy-eight wasn't nothing. People still basically liked me. Lacey still liked me.

Thank goodness I hadn't told her the truth.

Chapter Twenty-Two

JAZ WASN'T ON THE BUS come Monday morning. I was so used to her presence in the back seat that to see it empty was kind of a shock. A couple of the sixth graders quickly plunked themselves onto her place, then bounced back up again, as though she was somehow watching and might swoop in and destroy them.

She really wasn't there, though. I had to remind myself that, historically, Jaz had always had a pretty relaxed attitude to things like attendance and learning. Her absence didn't necessarily mean anything.

I guess I was particularly sensitive about things because everyone was being a little odd. Toward me.

It started with a sixth-grade girl smacking me with her bag as we got onto the bus, in a way that could have been an accident but clearly wasn't. After that, no one said anything to me at all. Fin didn't even bother trying to shake his empty bag of chips over my head. I guess I should have been grateful.

Only, coming off my weird weekend, I guess I was just feeling a little uneasy. Mom and Adrian were being so relentlessly positive that I could barely look at them. Dad, meanwhile, jumped out of his seat every time I came into the room, like he was waiting for me to catch on fire or melt down, and Amanda, well, I'd barely seen her. I was really looking forward to getting to school, which is saying something.

As I walked through the door of the classroom, I heard someone say:

"Here she is."

And someone else say:

"This is going to be interesting."

And then Paige and Sofie just came at me like they were a pair of pigeons and I was a potato chip:

"Katie, it's…?"

"What are you…?"

Then they ran out of words.

"Can someone please tell me what happened?"

Silence. The whole class just stared.

"Someone? *Anyone?*"

The crowd parted to reveal Savannah, her beautiful face looking beautifully pale.

"We saw. Don't try to deny it, Katie. We all know."

Holding out her gold-plated phone like it was some kind of religious offering, she began to walk toward me with these slow steps that seemed designed to make me want to scream. Luckily, I didn't have to wait the five minutes it would have taken for her to get to me. I just leaned forward and snatched it.

HYPOCRITE

In her latest single, teen sensation Katie Cox tells us that she hates boy bands.

But we know better.

An unnamed source, speaking exclusively to *Pop Trash*, told how Cox, watching from the wings of the Karamel concert, laughed, smiled, clapped, and sang to lead singer Kurt Thorpe, before engaging in a long and personal chat with him just after the show ended. Whatever she's been telling her fans, Ms. Cox clearly has ideas of her own.

The revelations come after what was billed by Top Music as the greatest chart battle in twenty years, between Cox's brand of "real" music and the more processed sound so beloved of Karamel's fans. Thorpe took to social media to state, "Peace and love to all our fans who bought the single and to all who bought Katie Cox's song," while Cox's account carried the message, "Karamel—u guys still suck."

Despite her strong words, in her interview with NTV News, Cox appeared unsettled. Clearly coming so close to her idols left the young singer-songwriter a little hot under the collar.

With her single languishing at the bottom of the charts, we ask, is now the time for Katie Cox to come clean about her deception? Her remaining fans obviously deserve the truth.

"Yeah." I looked up from the phone to see Lacey right in front of me. She was gripping Savannah's hand. "I think a little bit of truth would be nice."

"But…where…how did they…who…?"

"That's today's *Pop Trash*," said Paige, who I think thought she was being helpful. "And it's on TMZ too, and Mail Online and Jezebel. And E! And Perez Hilton did this whole thing… I'll send it to you if you want."

"It's not true," I said hopelessly. It was, after all, absolutely true.

"You lie, and you lie, and you lie," said Lacey.

"I…"

"It explains so much!" She was talking more to herself than she was to me. "Why you were humming 'Clap Your Hands' in the bathroom last week. Why you didn't invite me to their concert with you. Why you wanted me to come over and play all their songs."

I couldn't speak.

"And you told *Jaz*?"

I still couldn't speak. Instead, I found myself looking down at my wrist and fiddling like crazy with my birthday charm bracelet, as if there was a chance that some tiny chunks of silver might save me, which there was no way they could.

"I don't want you wearing that," said Lacey. "Take it off."

Everything seemed to go dark.

"It's very hard," said another voice. "I mean, obvs, I've known Katie for a while, and we're in the same class. But I think my loyalties have to be with my boyfriend Kolin because he is very upset and completely blameless, and he is my boyfriend so I do need to be there for him right now, since he is my boyfriend. Also, Katie is clearly rotten to the core."

"You're a very loyal person, Savannah."

"I know. I can't help it."

A buzz of conversation around me and then Ms. McAllister's voice: "Good morning, everyone. Savannah, that skirt is not even close to regulation length. I would ask you take it off, but I doubt I'd notice. Please go to the office right now and ask for something from lost and found. And someone catch Katie. She is clearly about to faint."

Then I was on the floor, my teacher's face filling my vision. "Katie?"

"I'm all right," I said.

"You are gray," said McAllister. "Lacey, take Katie to the nurse's office."

"No," said Lacey.

"Wh—oh, for goodness' sake. I will take her myself." Then, like she was Tarzan and I was Jane, McAllister lifted me into her arms. "The rest of you, assembly."

♪ ♫ ♫

It was Dad who drove me home, in a sleek silver car I hadn't seen before.

"A Honda Jazz, would you believe? And I asked for a brand-new BMW!"

"What? Where?" I was still having trouble forming sentences.

"Car rental. Your Adrian didn't seem to want me to

borrow his anymore, so I made the trip to Hertz." He thumped the wheel. "The joys of the open road!"

"Umph."

"You all right?"

"Er, not really. That's why I was sent home from school."

"I thought you were just faking!"

"No," I said. "I feel terrible."

"Don't puke on the upholstery, okay?"

"I won't."

I managed to stagger up the driveway and into my bedroom, Dad standing in the doorway.

"Can I get you anything, princess?"

I managed a laugh. "Did you see the stories?" After four tries, I managed to unhook the bracelet, and I dropped it onto my bedside table, where it sat in a sad little heap. "Maybe you could get me a new life."

He flapped a hand. "That garbage? Ignore it!"

"Dad…I can't."

"By this time tomorrow, everyone will have forgotten it." He patted his pocket. "Got to go, K. You take a little nap. Your mom'll be up soon."

I did try to sleep, but it's not easy at eleven in the morning, even for someone as good at it as me.

All I could think was that someone had betrayed me. Jaz? Jaz.

No wonder she hadn't come to school.

Only...

No, of course it was her.

Of course it was.

Can't believe u went to Pop Trash, Jaz.
I thought we were friends.

The message came back a moment later.

Can't believe you'd think I'd do that.
And I thought we were friends 2.

But...

U were the only one I told

Katie, read the article thoroughly. I wasn't at the concert was I?

I read it again. And—aargh—she was right.

An unnamed source, speaking exclusively to *Pop Trash*, told how Cox, watching from the wings of the Karamel

concert laughed, smiled, clapped, and
sang to lead singer Kurt Thorpe, before
engaging in a long and personal chat
with him just after the concert ended.

Jaz couldn't have known that.

Sry Jaz

No reply.

So if it wasn't Jaz, then it had to be someone else.

Of course. It was so obvious. I don't know why I'd ever
thought it was Jaz.

When it was Kurt.

He had seen me cheer for him. He knew I was still
releasing my song.

I'd betray me, under the same circumstances.

Only…when we'd talked, I guess I'd thought we had
some kind of connection, in a way I'd never really had with
a boy before. Scratch that. In a way I'd never really had
with anyone.

Which just made me hate him more. I opened my laptop.

KTCoX: Shocked Kurt_Karamel would sell me out
like that just 2 get his single to chart

In my head I could hear Amanda and Lacey telling me that I should step away from the keyboard. But only in my head. It wasn't like either of them was actually there.

I hit return.

> Kurt_Karamel: Nothing to do with me. But v glad to hear u r a fan ☺
> KTCoX: U sold me 2 the press
> Kurt_Karamel: I would never do that. You know I wouldn't.

Which did sort of feel true.

Then I caught myself. Never mind feelings. The point was, he had.

> KTCoX: I know what I see
> Kurt_Karamel: Out of line, Katie. You need to apologize right now
> KTCoX: U need to apologize. To me and to all of HUMANITY

Which felt pretty satisfying, I can tell you. What could he possibly come back with? I waited.

And waited. Then I refreshed.

And refreshed and refreshed.

And nothing. Except that, after a few seconds, his feed vanished.

He'd gone and *blocked* me! Which kind of said it all.

And I'd *trusted* him.

I let out a howl.

"What? Are you all right? Your father said you came home from school…"

Mom's head came poking around the door. She looked exhausted. Night shifts are always hard on her, but this was something worse.

"I felt a little funny," I said as she padded across the floor to feel my throat with warm fingertips.

"You'll live. Did you drink some water? Take some aspirin?"

I hadn't, but I nodded.

"This is about that story, isn't it? I've been getting messages all morning."

"Yes," I said. "But I'm okay. I am."

"Are you?"

"By this time tomorrow, everyone will have forgotten about it."

She folded her arms. "That's just the sort of thing your father would say."

"It's fine, Mom."

She looked at me strangely for a moment, as though

she was trying to decide whether or not to say something. Then: "Adrian called. Top Music asked if you might go in to see them about your album."

"Really?" I felt slightly better. No, a lot better.

A meeting, in that glass office, with the cookies and the black-and-white photos.

And most of all, a chance to go back and agree to record that song about partying late or kittens or whatever.

Because if that's what it would take to get back into Top Music's good books, I'd do it. Those lyrics they'd shown me weren't bad, not really, and a tune was even starting to suggest itself, a fast, rumbly set of chords, leading into a—

"Katie, this isn't good for you. I'm saying this as your mother. Stop now. It's gone too far."

"I said I'd stop when it was making me unhappy. And I'm happy! I'm really happy! I'm going to see my label. To plan my album!"

She gave me a quick kiss on the forehead. "I'm going to bed."

I stretched out and looked up, through my window and into the clouds.

Chapter Twenty-Three

KATIE! GREAT TO SEE YOU! Thanks for coming by on such short notice."

"That's okay. It wasn't like I was doing anything else," I said, and at the same time, Adrian said, "Good to see you, Tony."

We were standing in the lobby of Top Music, that glass ceiling slicing up the sunshine and throwing it down over us like liquid confetti.

"Okay, let's go on up," said Tony. "Did you get here all right? Traffic?"

"Took the train," said Adrian. "You know what the M25 can be like."

"I do," said Tony, in what was clearly one of the most boring conversations in human history. "I always say to Emma, it's worth having a decent car. We spend enough time in it."

"What you driving these days, Tone?"

"A Maserati—not as much fun as I'd like, but it does the job. You?"

Thank goodness I was so nervous, otherwise I'd probably have fallen asleep.

We sat down opposite Tony's enormous desk, with its collection of leather-framed photos: Tony and a pretty blonde lady on the deck of a boat, his shirt open and his tan deeper than ever; Tony and Karamel, on the stage of what looked like the *X Factor*; and a new one of Tony being interviewed by Chris on NTV News.

No cookies today, I noticed.

Tony leaned forward and fixed me with his gaze. "Well, now."

"Mmm."

"This is."

"Mm?"

We seemed to have gotten stuck just making noises at each other. I decided to nudge things along.

"Is…this…about the last few days?" I said.

"It is," said Tony. "How would you say it's been going?"

I sat up. "Well, not great, obviously."

Tony nodded, once then twice.

"So I guess the question is, what do we do next?"

I gave him what was supposed to be my most charming

smile. "It's clear that I'm not the best person to be in control of…me…so I'm willing to do whatever you tell me to do."

Under the table, I felt Adrian give my knee a squeeze. We both waited.

"Katie," said Tony. "Katie, Katie, Katie. You are really something, you know that?"

"Yes!"

"I've never met an artist quite like you. In fact, I've never met an artist anything like you."

Adrian gave me the tiniest of winks.

"You do go your own sweet way, don't you?"

"I do!"

"Look," said Tony. "The problem is this. Karamel are now at number one. And your single has dropped down to ninety-four. How can I put this? People don't buy music that's based on hate. They buy out of love."

"But…the iTunes chart won't include all the CD sales, will it? Adrian, you said you sold a few in the shop, and maybe other places have sold them too… I mean, some people still like me, right?"

"Maybe," said Tony. "But a handful of CDs won't change anything. You're not popular right now. Not with Karamel fans. And after recent *revelations*, not with Katie Cox fans, either. You're not popular with anyone."

"Maybe not in an obvious way. But changing your mind, it's not a bad thing. It's good, really, so if I just—"

"Katie, there's no arguing with the comments."

"But—"

Tony tapped something into his computer, and then, like he was some kind of magician or something and this was his final show-stopping trick, he swung the screen around.

There was me, at my concert, singing "Can't Stand the Boy Band." And underneath:

this is kinda mean

Katie Hater you are gonna be round for like maybe 1 month maybe too but Karamel will live 4 eva

My god this is shockingly bad and she looks AWFUL

Liar u said you hated Karamel but you love them u are full of LIES I don't trust u anymore I thought u were real but u are fake like all the rest

This song, her voice and face is disgusting. How did this get released?

this song made me vomit KRISTIAN I LOVE YOU I WILL NEVER STOP LOVING YOU

Disappointed. The whole thing is so low She should be fed to the sharks

Chart battle ROFL WE SLAYED YOU KATIE COX

Why is this happening? I dont understand no no no NO

Okay, I'm kind of tired of this. She needs to come back to what she was when she started out

Was Katie mad when she made the video? Her eyes are mad

it started out annoying, then got bad

Her first song was pure gold this is pure crap Last week I actually liked her now I hate her oh dear...

Back then she looked and dressed so much prettier but nowadays she doesn't

bad song bad attitude plus her face is GROSS

download song and play in reverse it is the devil speaking

already 320k dislikes well i disliked it too

I'm crying I thought u were real Katie but you love boy bands like all the rest

Her real name is Katie Plops hahahahaa

what is going on???? Duz she hate them or luv them? Dont undertsand

am i the only one who just want to cry in sadness because she is not who I thought

like come on

Trash music ugly girl GO AWAY STUPID SONG

So much hate, so many people, and it kept coming, more and more and more, and all I could think was that I didn't deserve this, that no one deserved this.

And that I should have been more sympathetic to poor Nicole when she'd been trolled back on the bus.

Back when it was all still okay. Before the end of the world.

My vision was beginning to blur, but I wouldn't let him know. I wouldn't let my voice even betray a hint of what I was feeling as I said, "So you think my next single should be something more positive? I can do that. I can totally do that."

"Positive is good," said Tony. "And I can't wait to hear it."

"Great!" I said. "I'll send something over as soon as I have it. Maybe even tonight!"

"If you like," said Tony. "But…Katie, we can't release it. The album isn't going to happen. You know that, don't you?"

"I…" I didn't.

"No one's denying your talent, but we think maybe you are not quite ready. For this. The music industry. You do understand."

Such small words, but each one so heavy. Like stones thrown into deep water. Down, down, down.

"I understand," I said.

"We've loved working with you. I'm sure our paths will cross again. When you're older."

"Of course," I said. "In fact, it's sort of what I was going to say anyway."

"Very wise," said Tony, getting to his feet in a way that said, *Leave now, Katie. I do not want you in my office anymore.*

And then there was mumbling about how the awards show dropped me, something about lack of representation by Tony, I wasn't on the list anymore, but I'd stopped listening.

Thank goodness for Adrian, sweeping me up in jackets and bags and a bunch of *Let's stay in touch* and *How's Emma, by the way?* All that middle-age stuff that I'd never understood the point of before—I could see now that it was for moments like this. All the garbage about housing prices and the weather and trains, I suddenly understood it was like bubble wrap or the foam pieces you get in packages: padding out the conversation, protecting the breakable thing sitting in the middle.

The broken thing. Me.

And all the while Adrian was talking, we were moving closer and closer to the door, and then we were in the elevator, and I made sure to keep my eyes away from the mirror so that while I could feel the tears on my face, I couldn't see them, and then finally, I was out in the street, the doors of Top Music closing behind me.

Conversational
Bubble Wrap

The store-brand version tastes just fine
Have you looked it up online?
Can't stay long, I have a meeting
Turn down your gas central heating

Adult talk is pointless crap
Conversational bubble wrap

Goodness me, I hate this weather
They are nice, are they real leather?
Want my problems? I've got plenty
Detour down the A120

Adult talk, let's recap
Is conversational bubble wrap

But some days life can be too real
Sometimes I'm afraid to feel
Please don't ask me how I've been
I'd rather chat about the queen

Fuel prices are monumental

Kids these days are going mental
Got to get back, trim our lawn
It's between the beige and fawn

But now I see my life's a trap
I think I want some bubble wrap

Chapter Twenty-Four

I GOT HOME TO FIND MOM surrounded by every shoe we'd ever owned, which was a lot of shoes.

"I'm clearing out the hall closet," she said as she crawled back into it.

"I see," I said. Then to her backside: "Top Music, they, er, dropped me."

She shot out backward. Like a champagne cork from a bottle of champagne, if the bottle was a closet and the cork was a butt.

"When…what…?"

"It doesn't matter."

She was pulling me toward her, and I felt the sadness coming, so I talked very fast. If I just made a wall of words, then maybe it wouldn't get through.

"I don't think I'm especially ready for any of this, and performing's not really my thing."

"I never liked that man," said Mom.

"Me neither," I said. "Well, honestly, I did, then I didn't, then I wasn't sure. Then I did. And now I don't."

"He should be protecting you," said Mom. "Not dropping you the second things get difficult."

"Maybe," I said. "But...they did get difficult because of me."

"Still," said Mom. "This is your chance, isn't it? To get back to normal." She tucked a strand of hair behind my ear. "I can't stand to see you so unhappy, Katie."

"I'm not..." I began. And then, because there was no way I could even begin to pretend that I was happy about any of this, I said, "I'll think about it. I promise."

She didn't say anything, but her hug told me that, finally, I was on my way to doing the right thing.

"Is there anything for dinner?" I asked her shoulder.

"Leftover Chinese," she said. "Top shelf of the fridge. Your father went a little overboard last night."

Eventually I blew my nose and went to investigate the food situation, leaving her in a mountain of old rain boots.

I mean, I do know I should have helped or something, but there's getting back to normal, and then there's clearing out the hall closet. I wasn't going to be *that* normal.

♪ ♫ ♩ ♬

And then I had to tell Mands.

"Just so you know," I said as we lay in the dark, failing to sleep. "It's all over, and I'm not a pop star anymore because Top Music doesn't want me because everyone hates me. Just so you know."

I heard her sit up. "I saw that it was all going badly… I'm sorry."

"It's fine. I'm thinking I'm done with it all, anyway."

We lay there in a silence that was intense.

I think Mands must have felt it too, because she put her light on and said, "Wanna hear something good? There's this band I found called New York Scandal. They're these four guys from Hull. They're playing at the shop. I think you'll really like them…their story is so inspiring…"

"Maybe I don't want to be inspired."

"So they do this great riff. I've never heard anything quite like it. Or maybe I have now that I think of it. They're kind of Daft Punk, in a funny kind of way, only more acoustic…"

And as she spoke, I saw how I'd never be free.

Music isn't just something you occasionally go and do.

It was everywhere.

Winding itself through my family and my friendships and my laptop and my phone.

If I wanted to be free, if I wanted to be normal, then

there couldn't be any more listening to gig recordings and there couldn't be any more jamming sessions. Or guitar lessons. Or new albums or karaoke or afternoons at Vox Vinyl flicking through the racks.

Because if I did that, then the next thing would be picking up my guitar, my shiny new guitar, and then I'd be writing songs, and that's what got me into this disaster in the first place.

If I wanted to be normal, if I wanted to be like Paige and Sofie and Savannah and Lacey, if I wanted to be *happy*, then I'd have to cut out every last little piece.

"Not tonight," I said to Amanda.

"You're right. It's late…"

"And not tomorrow morning, either."

She rubbed her eyes. "I thought you cared about this stuff, K. The shop, my gigs…"

"Sorry, Mands. I did. But I'm…just…finished."

We lay there for a minute, maybe two. My head was full to overflowing with thoughts, and my stomach was just the same, only with chicken-shrimp chow mein. Which reminded me.

"By the way, Dad said to give you this." I tossed Mands the little box, which she caught and then held. Then she let slip to the floor.

"I don't want anything from him. He—"

"Gave Mom over two thousand dollars." That got her. "Did he?"

"Yes! Plus, he bought us really good Chinese takeout. There's still some in the fridge, I think." Then I remembered. "No, I finished it. But he's really trying to make things right."

"It's not enough. He's…"

"Our father. And he's trying to make up for everything. I told him that he needed to start paying his way. Like you said. And he spoke to Catriona, even though he didn't want to, and he got the money back that he'd lent her for her stupid Pilates studio, and he gave it to Mom."

"Good. That's exactly what he should have done. A while ago."

I hesitated. But I'd come this far. "If he can do that, can't you at least give him a chance?"

"I don't want his jewelry," said my sister. "And it's going to take more than a little bit of money—"

"Over two *thousand* dollars! He can't do anything right, can he?"

"As far as you're concerned, he can't do anything wrong," said Amanda, turning off the light.

So I rolled over and went to sleep. Which wasn't the easiest, given the amount of leftover Chinese food I had to digest, but I managed.

Unfortunately I then got up an hour later to drink a gallon of water.

And an hour after that to pee.

Leftover Chinese Takeout Blues

I'm suffering, baby
I got food remorse
Oh I'm suffering, baby
Of silver carton food remorse
I guess I should've held back
On the sweet and sour sauce

I got them blues
Got them leftover Chinese takeout blues

Lying on my side
Feeling incredibly full
Whoa, I'm lying on my side
Feeling incredibly full
I guess all I can say is
Shouldn't have had that duck spring roll

I got them blues
Got them leftover Chinese takeout blues

Trying to sit up
In unbearable pain

Yes, trying to sit up
And I'm in the most unbearable pain
Shouldn't have finished off
All the chicken-shrimp chow mein

I got them blues
Got them leftover Chinese takeout
blues
But if I could live this evening over
I know I'd do the same again

Chapter Twenty-Five

So, WHAT DO YOU KNOW, I only woke up with the *best* idea for a song. It was called "Leftover Chinese Takeout Blues." The words were ready and waiting. I had my new guitar tucked under my arm and was just getting to grips with the chords when I remembered.

No more music.

I stuck the guitar back into its case and shoved it under my bed, and by the time I'd finished breakfast, I'd almost managed to forget about it.

What was harder was fighting the need to stick my headphones in my ears and have some Lana del Rey to take me down the lane. You have to be in a very specific mood for Lana—and when you are, it's extremely important to put her on right away before it passes.

Only, I wasn't doing music anymore.

Instead, I listened to the traffic and the birds and the wind, and they were just as good.

Almost as good. They were fine.

Jaz was at the bus stop, talking to Nicole. She didn't look at me.

"Morning," I said.

Nicole nodded. Jaz didn't say anything at all. I tried again. "What's the goss?"

I don't know where I got the word *goss*.

"We're talking about the dance," said Jaz.

"Ooh, great! That totally fits in with my new normal life. Because I'm not a pop star anymore. I'm a normal person who does stuff like going to the dance."

"*Me and Nicole* are talking about the dance," said Jaz, and then she turned her back on me.

Hmm.

Later in our classroom, things weren't much better. Lacey was sitting deep in the Savannah Zone, and I had to battle through a wall of Prada Candy before I got to a conversation that went: "It's the biggest shame that my boyfriend Kolin can't come to the dance. He has this awards thing at Wembley that night. It's so annoying, but what can I do? I have to be supportive of him because of how he's my boyfriend."

"Hey, Lace," I said. "So. Dance chat! What are you going to wear? Should we go to the thrift store?"

Lacey looked at me like I was a fly that had landed on a glazed doughnut she was about to eat.

"I should think that someone like you has better places to shop."

"No!" I had to stop myself from grabbing her by the shoulders. "I'm being normal again! Completely boring and music free!"

"Like me," said Lacey.

"Yes! I gave up the whole pop star thing. It wasn't exactly working out. I'm going to get back to doing ordinary person stuff. Like shopping at the thrift store. And going to the dance. You'll come with me, won't you, bestie?"

"Actually, I'm going solo," said Lacey.

"We can still go together," I said.

"I'm going solo with Savannah."

"Oh. Right."

And then I had an idea.

"Well, that's fine actually. You should go with Savannah. Because…I'm going to ask Dominic Preston!"

Going to the dance with a boy. Now that *was* normal.

"If you like," said Lacey.

"I do like! Him! Which is why I'm going to ask him."

"He's over there," said Paige helpfully.

"Later," I said. This was all moving a little fast. "I'm going to ask him later."

"Why not now?" said Sofie.

"Because of assembly."

"Assembly's not for ten minutes," said Paige. "Hey, Dom? Katie has something to ask you."

And the four of them turned and stared at what was turning into the Katie Cox Humiliation Show.

Dominic Preston slid down off the desk and came over. He really was very good-looking. Long and lean, with nice dark eyes, and hands that looked as though they'd be smooth and warm, not wet and trembly, like mine.

"Hey, Katie. Wassup?"

"Nothing," I said.

"But you just said you were going to—" Lacey began.

"Okay. Okay! Um, Dominic Preston. I wondered—" I began before clearing my throat and starting again, a lot lower. "I just wondered, whether you'd like to come to the dance. With someone. That someone being me."

Those good-looking eyes blinked. "We don't really know each other."

"No. But…"

"I'm not sure the dance's exactly the place for a first date."

"No," I said, wanting the earth to open up and…not *swallow* me, because that would be terrifying…but maybe hold me for a little bit until everyone had left and then let me out again. "No. You're right. I'm sorry. I—"

"We should go out first. Get to know each other."

"Really?" I cleared my throat. "That would be—" *Don't seem too eager. Don't seem too eager.* "Fine."

"Thursday night?"

Mom and Adrian would be at karaoke. "Sure."

"The Harvester Restaurant, okay? Seven o'clock?"

"Great!"

Then the bell rang for assembly, and I did my very best to look normal, which I completely was.

♪ 🎵 🎵

So the rest of the day unfolded in a normal way, except for not having anyone want to sit next to me in any classes or at lunch, and except for the part where Jill, my guitar teacher, came to ask me why I didn't go to my lesson, and I had to explain that I was no longer going to play the guitar, and I found myself getting surprisingly upset. It didn't last beyond the end of the double cheeseburger that I ate to cheer myself up again, though, so that was all right.

Best of all, when I came out at three thirty, there, parked right across that zigzag area that you're not supposed to park on, was Dad!

"Hop in, darlin'."

I hopped in.

"This is nice! How come you're here?"

"Just thought you deserved a bit of a treat."

"*I do*," I said. "Everything's been so"—*don't bring things down, Katie*—"annoying, recently."

"Your mother said. Want to talk about it?"

"There's not much to say. I was a pop star. Now I'm not."

"You'll always be a star to me," said Dad.

"Great," I said, starting to turn the radio on, maybe find some Jay-Z to lift the mood, and then remembering I wasn't doing that anymore and folding my hands back into my lap.

"So"—Dad spun the wheel—"when you were in there. Top Music. At the office...did Tony say anything about me?"

"What?" I held my breath as we squeezed past a street sign, where Mands had once lost a side mirror. "When?"

"When you saw him. Did Tony mention my demo?"

"We didn't really get to that."

"Oh. And you don't think you could ask?"

"Um, maybe." I thought about it. "Actually, probably not. No."

"Right."

A flare of annoyance, like a match being lit, sparked in me. It had been pretty much the worst ten minutes of my life, in that room, and now Dad wanted me to make it about him? Then, like always when I light matches, the feeling sputtered out again. He needed a job. I'd said I'd help him. And I hadn't.

I decided to change the subject.

"Anyway. I've got some news, Dad. I'm going on a date. My first date."

He'd been looking thoughtful, screwing up his face in the sun, but now he sat up straight and revved the engine so hard that the driver in the van next to us gave me a funny look.

"My baby is going on her first ever date!"

"He's called Dominic Preston, and he's really gorgeous. We're going to the Harvester."

We pulled up onto the driveway, and he stopped the car. "Now, Katie, have we ever talked about the birds and the bees?"

Oh boy.

"Yes, Dad. Not you and me—but I have had that talk."

Thank goodness for Amanda. How people cope without big sisters, I do not know.

"Well," said Dad, "don't do anything that I wouldn't do."

"Dad."

"Anyway, I guess there's a limit to what you can get up to in a Harvester. Although, there was this one time, in a Taco Bell, I'd just started seeing Catriona and—"

"*Dad.*"

"Maybe I'll save that one for when you're older."

Chapter Twenty-Six

I'D BEEN HOPING FOR TIME to do some pre-date psyching myself up, but after a full-scale disaster involving nude tights, a run in one leg, and a bottle of red nail polish, I was running seriously late. I got off the bus and found that he was already there, standing by the door, fiddling with his phone.

He seemed different, away from school. Taller. Older.

Stay calm, I told myself. *What's the worst thing that could happen?*

My imagination immediately responded with one word: *diarrhea*.

"Katie! Hi!"

He saw me as I was crossing the road. I did a small wave.

"Hello, Dom. In. Ic."

"Call me Dom?"

His voice was friendly and nice-sounding, and as I got closer, close enough to give him a sort of air kiss on the cheek and smell his deodorant, it occurred to me that I'd never had an actual conversation with the guy. I didn't know anything about him at all.

Beyond the fact that he was gorgeous, of course. "Ready to go in?"

"I was thinking we could maybe sit outside," I said, and we looked at the Harvester's picnic tables, which were lined up next to the parking lot and facing the very busy main road, and then up at the heavy sky. "Nah, that was a bad idea. Let's not."

"We can if you want?"

"No, it's fine."

"If you want to sit outside, we should sit outside."

"I don't want to sit outside."

He stepped backward.

"I mean…inside would be great," I said.

Inside was dark, with shiny red leather chairs and menus that were a little sticky. We sat down at a table near the bar and under a speaker. The stereo was playing something catchy but faint, and I strained to hear it above the rattle of the till.

It was…oh, man, it was Karamel.

The restaurant dissolved, and I was standing by the side of the stage again, watching Kurt dip his head in concentration as all of the O2 screamed.

No. No, no, no. This would not do. This would not do *at all*.

I needed to be focusing on Dominic Preston, who was *here* and *gorgeous*, unlike Kurt, who might have been a tiny bit good-looking and maybe slightly talented and who seemed to really get me, *but* he had sold me out to the press and was not even been big enough to admit it and anyway had understood the old musical Katie, not the new, normal one.

"Excuse me," I said to the woman behind the bar. "Is there any chance you could play something else?"

She gave me a funny look, then walked off. A second later and we were listening to Rihanna.

"So," said Dominic Preston, smiling at me over the menu, clearly not having noticed my mini meltdown, or if he had, being too polite to mention it. "So."

"So!" I said, thinking, *Be normal*. "What's your favorite food? Mine's roast beef. But they only do that on Sundays. So I guess I'll have a burger."

"Two burgers," said Dominic to the woman behind the bar, and I have to say, I got a little tingle at the thought that I was on a date with someone who liked burgers as much as me, i.e., a lot.

There was a long silence. Long enough for me to clock that the stereo had stopped playing "We Found

Love" by Rihanna and started playing "Umbrella," also by Rihanna. Long enough to count how many other people were there, which was twelve, not including waiters, and thirteen including them. Long enough to notice that time was slowing down and that the second hand on the clock above the bar was actually creaking around, and I still didn't know what I was going to say, and I really should say *something*.

> Message from Katie's mouth to Katie's brain: Hey there. Any possible conversation topics you might want to throw me here?
> Katie's brain: Diarrhea?
> Katie's mouth: Okay, that's great, thanks brain, thanks very much.

"Umbrella" ended, and "Red" by Taylor Swift started up, and maybe it was just getting some much-needed Tay fierceness into my ears, but I finally had the courage to stop pretending this was all fine and say:

"Sorry, this is weird. We don't know each other at all. I shouldn't have…this is a bad idea. Should I go? I'll just go. Maybe bring my burger to school tomorrow. I'll have it cold for lunch."

"Katie!" His hand was on mine. "Don't… I know it's

weird. And yeah, we don't know each other. But I've liked you for, well, forever."

"You have?"

He looked down at the table, and I thought how very gorgeous he was, those long eyelashes brushing his cheeks, the way his chin…was.

"Yeah. You must have noticed."

"Not really. But, um, yay."

We grinned, and everything seemed a little better. "So. What's it like being famous then?"

"Oh"—I scrunched my napkin—"I'm not doing that anymore. My contract got canceled. It's all over."

"No!"

"Yes. But I wasn't really down with the whole celebrity thing anyway. Let's talk about other stuff. Where do you live? Have you always been in Harltree?"

"But you're still going to get lots of money from that song you did, aren't you?"

"I don't know. So we used to live on the other side of Harltree, and then after my parents split up, near the fields in this crazy falling-apart house. I hated it for a long time, but now I think I maybe don't hate it quite as much as I did. Although I do still hate it. You?"

"I'm not very interesting," said Dominic.

"Of course you are!"

"Not as interesting as you. Who's the most famous person you've ever met?"

The answer was obviously Kurt, but I wasn't going to say that. "I chatted with Crystal Skye once at a thing, but it wasn't really that exciting."

Our burgers arrived, which was good, because I really like burgers. He didn't seem particularly happy about his. After about three minutes of frenzied eating on my side of the table and a bit of poking around on his, I said, "Not hungry?"

"I'm okay."

"Because this is really good," I said, managing to squirt burger juice down my front. "Go on. Eat some."

"I'm…I'm sort of…a vegetarian," said Dominic.

"Oh. You could go to the salad bar if you want. I think it comes free with any main course."

"Are you going?"

I laughed so loudly that an old man at the bar gave me a look. "I'm not really a salad person."

"Then I'm fine," said Dominic.

"Why did you order a burger?"

"Because you did."

"Er, okay."

Was that an odd thing to do? This is the problem with first dates. You don't have anything to compare them to.

Maybe it wasn't odd. Maybe it was nice. After all, he was smiling at me and saying, "You're really cool, Katie."

"Am I? I mean, thank you. So, anyway, what kind of music do you like?"

He put his chin into his cupped hand and smiled. "*Your* music."

No, this definitely was kind of weird. But a good kind of weird. Definitely the good kind. "Thanks!" I said. "But other than that?"

"Oh, you know."

I'd finished my burger and was now down to the last few fries. Dominic had barely touched his. Not even the fries. Not even the fries that weren't touching the burger. He was just watching me with an intense expression.

Maybe this was chemistry.

"I don't!" I said. Maybe he was just shy. "Look, okay. So I'm majorly into Joni Mitchell right now and Adele. I know she's everywhere, but it's totally justified. She's this incredible talent, isn't she? And Feist. And Amy Winehouse. She only made two albums, but they're so perfect. Have you ever heard any Ella Fitzgerald? The way she sings, it gives me chills. And Billie Holiday, obviously. Lorde's pretty cool. And Caitlin Rose. And…" I was talking far too much. "Okay, now you say someone."

He coughed. "I…guess…I like…the Beatles."

"Yes! Me too! Which is your favorite album? Mine's probably *The White Album,* but I'm majorly into their earlier stuff too."

"I like *The Dark Side of the Moon.*"

"See, that's not actually a Beatles album," I said. "It's by Pink Floyd. But it is really good. I absolutely get why you'd choose it."

"Katie, will you go out with me?"

And there it was.

Normal life!

I was going to be Dominic Preston's girlfriend!

We'd go to the dance together and hang out and listen to *The Dark Side of the Moon.*

"Yes! That would be nice."

We linked hands across the table, and I hoped that he didn't mind mine being a little sticky and smelling of meat.

"And now, when you do concerts and stuff, I can come with you!"

"Yeah," I said. "Except I gave that up. Like I said—um, sorry, what are you doing?"

He had his phone up in the air. "Just taking a photo."

"Great. Why?"

"To show everyone. Because you're my girlfriend."

"Because I'm your girlfriend," I said, trying not to flinch as he took one, then three, then five photos, some of me, some of me and him, one of me and my empty plate. "Cool."

"So we should plan another date. Me and my celebrity girlfriend."

"Yes," I said, wondering why it was that another date with Dominic Preston wasn't sounding nearly as exciting as it would have even half an hour ago. "But look. I'm not this celebrity. I'm just like you, like everyone else at school. That's okay, isn't it?"

A new waitress came to take our plates, and as she did, she gave me a double take. "Aren't you…?"

"She's Katie Cox," said Dominic. "The one who got all those hits on her video. She had a number two single."

"Oh wow," said the waitress. "Will you sign…will you sign—" She looked around for something for me to sign. There wasn't anything. Even the menus were laminated. "My pad! Will you sign my pad?"

"I don't want to," I said. "I mean, I can, but I'm trying not to do that sort of thing. Sorry."

She took a step back. "I see. Think you're too good for us?"

"No! It's just…"

"I'll get your check." And she stomped off.

I was almost too shocked to cry. Almost. The tears wobbled on my lashes as I said, "Sorry, was that…? I only said that I didn't want to…"

"I guess that means you won't sign this, either," said Dominic, sliding a CD out of his pocket. It was "Just Me," still in its wrapper.

"I'd rather not," I said.

The check came smacking down onto the table. I got out a ten. He didn't move.

"Aren't you...this is all I have..."

"But you can afford to pay it," he said.

"I can't really. At least, not tonight."

Finally, he got his wallet out and put down a ten too. And then we were walking out, past the horrible waitress, who was watching me like I was made of solidified puke or something, and into the parking lot.

"Well, this has been—"

He was looking at me funny.

"Really great and everything. And—"

He was leaning in.

"And I'm so glad we did it, but—"

He was close now, so close, because, oh man, he was about to kiss me. Either that or he was examining my earrings.

No, he was tilting his head, and I could feel his breath. In fact, I could even smell it. This was definitely pre-kiss territory. I was about to experience my very first kiss. And—

"I'm sorry," I said. "I'm not sure I'm...that we're... I'm sorry."

He took a step back and half closed his eyes. Eyes that somehow didn't seem nearly as gorgeous as they had. "Is it because you only like celebrities now?"

"No! Just—"

"That waitress was right back there. I'm not good enough for you. None of us are good enough for you."

"No! That's not what…no!"

"Get lost, Katie Cox."

Chapter
Twenty-Seven

BUT...

But, but, but, but, but...

But...

My mouth formed the word, over and over again, only before I could finish, he was gone.

Even if he'd stayed, I don't know what I would have said.

He'd looked at me, the waitress had looked at me, and what had they seen? Not me, or at least, not the real me. They'd seen a version of Katie Cox, the girl who sang and played and grinned into her webcam. They hadn't seen the me who wanted to disappear.

My hand went for my phone. Mands didn't pick up.

Mom didn't pick up. Adrian didn't pick up.

Dad didn't even have his switched on.

Lacey, she screened me. I could tell because it rang five times. Just long enough for her to see who it was and hit

Ignore. So cruel. She could at least have let it go to voice mail *naturally*.

I didn't even stop to think about the last person I'd dialed until I heard her voice saying, "What?"

"Um, hi, Jaz."

"Go away."

"Okay!"

I put the phone down. It began to drizzle.

I redialed.

"What?"

"Jaz, I—"

"I told you to go away."

"All right." I hung up again.

The rain was really coming down now.

"What?"

"Jaz, can we do this face-to-face? I'm worried water's going to get into my phone, and it's not insured."

Jaz, it turned out, lived two streets away from me, which was a forty-five-minute walk from the restaurant, minimum. And I was wearing my red sandals—sandals that completely broke my usual shoe rule, which is that all footwear needs to be good for at least an hour of standing slash walking.

And all for Dominic Preston, who clearly hadn't noticed them.

In fact, I thought, as I made my way toward the underpass, I don't think he had noticed actual me at all.

So Dominic Preston was now officially off the radar. But that was all right. That still left lots of other people who liked the real normal me.

People like… People like…

People like the people on the Internet. Who thought I was stupid and gross and ugly and wrong. People who wanted me wiped off the face of the earth. On my phone and in my laptop and serving at the Harvester and in my class and going on a date, and I'd never be safe, never get to be just me ever again.

A sob tore at my throat.

In my head, Mom's voice: "Calm down, Katie. Calm down."

I'd been too ambitious. That was all. Obviously it would take longer than a couple of days to undo everything that had happened. The new normal Katie would come. I was just going to have to work a little harder. Harder on…what exactly?

What would normal Katie Cox do?

Watch TV. Do some messaging. Cleaning my room was pretty much a full-time job. I could do that. And let my thoughts flit away. There was really no need to capture them in my lyric book anymore. It wouldn't help.

The music though. Just talking about the *White Album*

back there had made my ears thirst for "While My Guitar Gently Weeps."

And Billy Joel! How would I live without Billy Joel? Or Jimi Hendrix? Or Dolly Parton or Amy Winehouse or Miles Davis? If there was ever a walk that needed the soundtrack of *Kind of Blue*, it was this one.

It was only now that I began to wonder. I could just about live without music for a day, even two. But those voices, the voices of my deepest feelings, the voices—even though I'd never meet them—of my friends...I'd have to live without them forever.

When I had pictured Jaz's house, it was pretty much exactly like the castle in *Dracula*. High on a hill, with turrets and bats, and in the center of a red, red room, a coffin, and in that coffin, Jaz.

Not a semidetached house with a porch and a stained-glass front door, opened by a smiling, plumpish woman with dyed blonde hair who said, "Jasmine's in her bedroom, upstairs, second door on the right."

"Okay," I said, putting my head down and heading for the stairs.

"It's great to meet you, Katie. Jasmine's always talking about you. She's really changed since the two of you've been friends, you know. Come out of her shell. We're so glad she found you."

"Er, yeah," I said.

I hadn't been expecting that, either. Or a beige carpet and a mishmash of framed pictures going up the stairs: baby Jaz; Jaz on a tricycle; Jaz in a bridesmaid's dress, smiling with gapped teeth.

Luckily, I opened her bedroom door onto what was basically a shrine to Marilyn Manson and saw Jaz scowling from somewhere in the middle of a black lace hooded dress thing covered in sequined grim reapers.

Phew.

"I've ruined my life," I informed her. "And now I'm paying for it, and I deserve it, I know I do, but I don't think I can take much more."

"You do deserve it," said Jaz.

"Oh, Jaz. I should never have accused you of selling that story. It's not your style."

"No. It's not."

"I mean," I said, wanting her to understand, "you are truly out there. But—"

"I don't lie," said Jaz. "I don't lie about what I believe."

"No," I said. "And from now on, I'm not going to, either."

She didn't seem convinced.

"Jaz, please. I'll give up Lacey and Karamel. But I cannot lose you too. You're amazing. I wish I could be more like you."

And were those *tears* I saw in her eyes?

"Enough melodrama." She pushed back her hair, and I realized I must have been mistaken. Eyes like Jaz's couldn't possibly cry. If nothing else, they were clearly too blocked up with eyeliner. "Drippy Lacey will come sliming back. And you love Karamel."

"I do not love them. I mean, I love their music. Loved it. But…Kurt sold me out. He said he forgave me and then he went to the press."

Jaz chewed, maybe a piece of gum, maybe just a complicated thought. "Maybe not," she said. "Did you at least consider that it was someone else?"

"No! It was him. Of course it was him."

"Then let's start by doing that. Who else was there? Who saw you? At the concert?"

"Um. That journalist, Chris."

"It's a good story. He would have reported it with his name. So it's not him."

"There were tons of backstage people. It could have been any of them."

"They would have signed stuff saying they wouldn't talk to the press. It's not going to be one of them."

"It has to be. Because the only other person is Dad, and it's not him."

"Why not?" asked Jaz.

"Because Dad wouldn't do that! He's not…he just wouldn't. Okay?" I wasn't convincing her. "He's my *dad*."

"Kurt from Karamel's dad sold stories about him," said Jaz. "There's lots of stuff floating around out there. Some people say that's what their second album's all about."

"How did you know that?" I asked. "And since when have you been into Karamel?"

"Couple of weeks," said Jaz. "But we're talking about you. And your dad."

"Look," I said. "Dad's had a few…issues. But we're talking about a man who gave Mom over two thousand dollars a few days ago. And it's not like he can exactly afford it."

Jaz leaned forward. "If he can't afford it, then where did he get two grand? From *Pop Trash*?"

"No! From Catriona. His ex-girlfriend. He loaned her some money. We had a talk. He got it back and gave it to Mom."

Jaz nodded at my phone. "Easy enough way to check," she said.

"I trust him," I said. "I am not calling Catriona."

Jaz didn't reply. And I looked at my phone, pictured Dad's face, and felt his arms around my shoulders, and I knew—100 percent knew—that he hadn't…this was Dad we were talking about…

I also knew what Amanda would say. Exactly what Amanda would say.

And that Amanda was wrong.

"If you know it wasn't him, if that's genuinely what you believe, then fine," said Jaz, and she looked as serious as I've ever seen her. "But if any part of you believes that it might have been him, then…you said you were going to tell the truth from now on, Katie. You just told me that."

"I…I don't have her number," I said. "She could be anywhere. Her and Dad split up, and I can't ask him, can I?"

"What do you know about her?"

"Nothing helpful. That she runs a Pilates studio in California. That her last name is something like Fernando or Ferdinand or—"

"Catriona Fernandez," said Jaz, looking triumphantly up from her phone. "Here's the number for her studio."

"But what if it's the middle of the night over there? What if she doesn't want to speak to me? Or she's in the middle of teaching a class. What if—" And then I had to stop talking because Jaz was shoving her phone to my ear, and I could hear ringing.

And then: "Poise Pilates, can I help you?"

"Um. Hi. I was just wondering if I could speak to Catriona, only she's probably not there, so never mind, I'll just—"

"Speaking. How may I help you?" She sounded

very American. Like she was in a movie or something. I thought, not for the first time recently, that my life didn't seem real anymore.

"Oh. This is…um…Katie. Katie Cox. Benjamin Cox's daughter. Sorry."

"You Brits, always apologizing. Hi there, Katie! Great to finally speak to you. How is Benji?"

"He's, er, okay."

"I'm so glad! He's a good guy, you know? Of course you do. He's your dad! And how can I help you, Katie?"

Jaz was looking at me, very, very hard, as I said, "Sorry. I mean, not sorry. But this is a little…" Jaz tilted her head. "Did Dad lend you some money?"

"He sure did, honey. I never asked. You know that? But he saw I needed a little help, and when the studio lease came up, there he was with the down payment. He's a generous guy."

I began to smile. It was all going to be okay. "He *is* generous, isn't he?"

"Didn't even ask for it back when we split."

"No?" My stomach began to turn.

"Nope! Not a single dollar. But I'm going to return every dime. The second we start turning a profit, I'm going to start paying him back. My mamma told me, Catriona, you don't ever stay in debt. Especially not to a man."

"Huh," I said.

"Oh, I'm so glad to be able to talk to you, Katie. Your dad, he was always so proud of you. Showing everyone your photo, telling anyone who'd listen about his baby girl. He loves you so much."

"Yeah," I said. "Um, I have to go now, Catriona."

"Send him my love, will you?"

"I will."

"Bye bye, honey pie."

I let the phone drop onto Jaz's bed.

"That doesn't mean he did it," I said. "He could have gotten the money anywhere. Maybe it was from work. An old job! He's always saying how they take forever to pay up. Maybe…maybe…oh no…no, no, no…"

"Stay there," said Jaz. "I'll get Mom to drive you home."

♪ ♫ ♪

It doesn't mean…

  Just because he didn't…

  He's not…

The house was empty. Everyone was out. Everyone except—

"Dad?"

He had the fridge open, and when he heard my voice, he turned, his face bathed with a sickly yellow light. "Katie!" My eyes must have given away some of what I was feeling because he peered at me and said, "What?"

"Dad. That story about me at the Karamel concert. That's…everywhere. Did it…did it come from you?"

Please. Please say no. Please say something. Please.

"D-Dad?"

His silence said it all.

"How could you, Dad? How *could* you?"

"I was out of cash. You were saying your mother needed rent."

"So, couldn't you, I don't know, get a job or something?"

"It's not…my phone has not been ringing much recently. Haven't had a dry spell like this in a while." He looked up. "Have you had a chance to speak to Tony?"

Dad's never been especially good at reading a situation. This, though, this took things to a whole new level.

"A few days in the studio would work things out. See if you can't get me in, okay?"

"Dad, you sold a story about me!"

"They only wanted a quick chat, about you and what you were up to. It was such a great evening. What's wrong with that?"

"*What's wrong with that?* Don't you even…I mean, it

was a Karamel concert...I wasn't supposed to be having a good time."

"Weren't you? Then why were we there?"

"Dad, do you have any idea what's been going on these last few days? With my life? Any idea at all?"

"Don't you like your new guitar?"

"Of course, but I..."

"Because I remembered," he said, like some kitten I was kicking in the face. "You said that was the guitar you wanted."

"*That's* what you took from the concert? You knew what I had to say about Karamel, and you went and sold me out, and you think you can make it okay with a stupid new guitar? Didn't...didn't you even hear my song?"

"Of course I did! I loved it! I'm so proud of you."

And, oh, a part of me still thrilled to hear him say it. "You shouldn't have done it, Dad."

"I couldn't live off that man's charity."

"But why didn't you ask for the money back from Catriona?"

He looked away. "Allow a man some dignity, Katie." Then, in a single beat, I hated him.

"And you let me blame poor Kurt," I said. "You let me go online and tell the whole world it was him, when all the time it was you?"

He was laughing now. "*Poor Kurt?* I'm not going to feel too sorry for him, thank you very much!"

I thought I might…I don't even know. Punch a wall or be sick. Because Amanda was right. She'd been right from the start.

"Katie? Katie!"

"I thought you cared about me," I said. "I thought I mattered. But you only care about you."

My voice must have cracked or something because he stopped laughing.

"These past few weeks, I've been defending you! To Mom, to Amanda… It's like, you destroyed the family once, and now you're coming back to do it all over again." I thought he'd deny it. Instead, he bowed his head.

"That's fair," he said. "I let you all down. I know that."

"If you know that, then why did you…?"

"I let you all down," he repeated. "If I could go back and do things differently, then I would. But I can't."

I was backing away from him now, knowing I couldn't breathe even a molecule of air that had passed through his lungs.

"Katie, how do you think it feels, to have to go begging to your daughter? Can we not just…"

"No," I said. "In fact…" I got out my phone.

Hi, Tony

It's Katie.

So, I lied to you, about Dad being unreli-
able because I didn't want him to go away. But
if there's still a job on that Papaya album, you
should give it to him. I think you owe me that.

I won't bother you again.

Katie

"There," I said. "I'll get you some work. With Tony."

"I—I don't know what to say."

I did. "Go to America. And this time, don't come back."

Chapter Twenty-Eight

NANDS FOUND ME SITTING ON the floor. I don't know what time it was, but it must have been late. It was dark outside, and when she came past me, I could smell the night air in her hair.

I say "found." What I mean is that she tripped over my right arm and went flying.

"What on earth are you doing there?"

"Sorry. I was just…sorry." I rubbed my elbow. "Where were you?"

"Since when do you care?"

She snapped the light on, and I had to shield my eyes. "Wuh?"

She took her jacket off angrily and sat down on her bed. "You're the one who's completely wrapped up in her own little world. 'Oh, I'm a pop star. I'm dating. I'm hanging out with Super Dad…' What? Why are you looking at me like that?"

"It was Dad," I said. "Not Kurt. It was Dad. He sold me out. For money. It was always Dad."

She tensed. Then she said, "Of course it was. Oh, Katie." Then she held me while I cried. It was a long time.

She didn't say, "I told you so." She didn't remind me how Dad had ducked out of coming to see me sing solo at the school Christmas concert when I was nine because he got a last-minute spot on a TV show. She didn't mention that, three years ago, he'd set his heart on a vintage guitar, a handmade Benedetto Fratello and, in order to buy it, had sold our car. And she didn't say anything about how he'd been too much of a wuss to tell Mom he was coming back, how he'd left it to me, and then sold me out and ruined everything.

Or maybe it was already ruined, and I just hadn't noticed.

Funny how it takes being pressed face-first into a denim jacket to get some perspective on things.

Finally, Amanda spoke. "I've got a chocolate bar in my bag."

"A raisin one?" My voice sounded weird. Croaky and soft. Like someone else's.

"A raisin one, yes. You never change, you know that, Katie?"

We shared it, and I felt, not better, exactly, but at least stable.

"Everyone hates me," I said.

"You're being absurd."

"I'm not. Dominic Preston just told me to get lost. Kurt blocked me. Lacey called me a liar." I picked up the charm bracelet, then let the cold metal slip between my fingers, back onto my bedside table. "I *am* a liar."

"Okay, but…"

"And the only people who hate me more than Karamel fans are the Katie Cox fans. Ex-fans." I put my head in my hands. "Maybe I need a new identity. Do you think I qualify for a witness protection program? Or a new face?"

For a second, I thought how, actually, a new face might be really nice, how I could maybe get a smaller nose, one of those ski-slope ones like Savannah has, and really white teeth.

I could ask them to make my eyes not look quite so much like Dad's too.

"What I don't understand is where all this hate came from in the first place," said Amanda.

Wasn't it obvious?

"It's music," I said. "Music keeps people apart. It divides people. That's what it does."

"No, it doesn't."

"It does! That's what I've realized. That's where everything started. If it hadn't been for music, I'd still be friends with Lacey, I wouldn't have the entire population of the universe wanting to kill me, and Mom and Dad would probably still be together!"

Amanda shook her head. "That is the biggest pile of garbage I've ever heard."

What?

"What?"

"Of course it's not music's fault. Music is"—her face worked as she struggled to get her feelings into words— "music is the best thing. It's the only thing. It's everything."

"No."

She went to the stereo and put on Irma Thomas's "Good Things Don't Come Easy." Irma's voice filled the room and filled up my heart. For a long time, we just listened.

"I thought, if I just stopped playing, that would be enough," I said into the thick silence that followed. "It's over. So why isn't it over?"

"Because it isn't," said Amanda.

Somehow, I knew that she was right.

♪ ♫ ♫

"Okay then," said Jaz.

It was the next morning, and the Katie Emergency Committee—i.e., the very few people in the world who could still stand to look at me—was sitting around the table having breakfast.

The fact that we were there at 8:00 a.m. just goes to show how big an emergency it was.

Adrian cleared his throat, this long, flappily wet noise that made me remember that I'm never going to smoke, and said, "What can we do?"

"We can't do anything," said Amanda.

"What can we do to help?"

"Nothing," I said. "The entire world thinks I'm a complete idiot, and they're right. I can't go near Lacey, and even if I could, what am I going to say to her? Plus, I accused Kurt…" I couldn't even finish that one.

"So tell him who it really was," said Amanda. "And that you're sorry."

"I should." Then I thought about it for more than half a second and plunged even further into my pit of despair. "But I can't. There's no way."

"That one seems easy enough to figure out." Adrian took a glug of cold coffee. "Can't you just send him a message? Through one of your websites?"

"No," I told him. "He blocked me."

"Are you sure?"

I unlocked my phone and scrolled through, but there was no Kurt. Instead, I just got a load of Paige and Sofie and Lacey, rattling on about getting a pre-dance manicure, and how orange was the color to go for because of how it went with everything or didn't go with anything or something. They were getting tons of likes, so clearly some people were finding it useful.

"He's gone," I said. "And anyway, I think maybe this is one of those conversations it's better to have in private. If I told him online, it would be like I was saying it just so that everyone else could hear."

"You'll have to stalk him," said Jaz. "Go to a concert. Turn up in his dressing room. You're still famous enough for them to let you in."

I put my phone back down on the table. If Lacey wanted to paint her fingers a color called Satsuma Sunset, that was her business. "I can't turn up at a Karamel concert. They'll eat me."

I waited for someone to disagree, to tell me that I was being over the top, that it would be fine. No one did.

"Anyway their tour's over. They're not playing in the UK again. Not for I don't know how long."

"They are," said Jaz, looking at her screen. "They're playing tonight at the Teen Time Awards."

Which rang a bell, somewhere at the back of my head. "The Teen Time Awards. That's at…"

"Wembley," said Amanda. "So we have to go to Wembley. At six o'clock. Oh *damn*."

"What?"

"It's gig night at the shop. But you know what? I'll cancel. If forty people wanted to come tonight, they'll want to come again next week."

"Forty? So we're sold out?" said Adrian, and I remembered all over again how hard he and Amanda had worked to make that place a success. And how I'd told her that I didn't care about the shop. Or her gigs. Great stuff, Katie.

"Yeah, it's been sold out since yesterday," said Mands. "But you're more important."

"No," I said, suddenly desperate. "I'm not. You can't cancel gig night. But…I'll miss you."

"I should hope so," said my annoying, sanctimonious, *brilliant* big sister. "Okay."

"So you have to go to Wembley Arena and go backstage and then get into Kurt's dressing room." She made it sound as easy as a trip to the grocery store.

"Er, how?"

"Can't your record label…?" began Jaz.

"No, they dropped me."

"So find another way."

"Give up, Jaz. It's impossible." I flicked my phone on again to see Paige's face beaming next to a large and sparkly shoe.

"We need some kind of connection," said Amanda. "A way into the band."

"But there isn't one!" I refreshed, and got a picture of a Prada label next to a sad face emoji and the words, "*Sooo upset I have to go to the dance tonight without my beautiful boyfriend.*"

"Will you please put your phones away?" said Adrian. "It's like talking to a pair of zombies! Honestly, when I was your age…"

"I know," said Amanda. "You wouldn't think this was something they cared about, would you? Hold on. What? What is it?"

My eyes met Jaz's. "Savannah."

Chapter Twenty-Nine

I HAD TO WAIT OUTSIDE THE manicure place for what felt like forever. Then, just as I was about to give up and go crawl into bed and never come out, they all turned up together, wobbling a little on the cobblestones because even Lacey had put her heels on early. Which, if you ask me, was a major error with the whole dance still ahead, but let's be clear, literally no one was asking me.

Then they saw me and stopped.

My hand was in my pocket, so Lacey couldn't see the charm bracelet. It was there, though, around my wrist, reminding me that I'd once had a best friend.

"Hello, Savannah!" I sang, trying to appear as carefree as possible. "Afternoon, Sofie. Hey, Lace. Hi, Paige! You look nice. I like your…skin."

"Thanks, Katie," said Paige, who in fact does have very good skin, although it wasn't looking much different from how it normally did.

"What are you even doing here, babes?" said Savannah. "This is a *beauty* salon."

"I know. But I was thinking about what you said. About how I'm rotten to the core and stuff, and I thought maybe, if I got a little more graceful and pretty, it might make me a better person. You know?"

I could barely make sense of what was coming out of my own mouth. Only then, Savannah nodded very seriously and said, "Maybe. You know what they say. Beauty starts on the outside."

I moved between her and the door.

"So here's the thing, Sav. I just found out that I won a bag."

"That's great, babes. But I'm going to be late for my nail appointment. So—"

"A designer bag. By, er, Gucci."

She stopped and stood a little straighter. I was reminded of how tigers act when they see baby gazelles. Yes, Savannah was practically sniffing the air.

"It's so random," I went on. "I entered this competition forever ago, one of those email ones, you know. And the next thing I know, this delivery guy is knocking on the door with a Gucci bag!"

"Uh-huh." She was leaning in.

"And here's the thing," I said. *"I don't even like it!"*

"That is understandable," said Savannah. "You are not

really a Gucci kind of a girl, Katie. And that bag, it deserves a Gucci kind of a girl."

"Exactly," I said. "So I was wondering, could you come and take a look at it? Tell me what to do? Maybe you know someone who might like it…?" I glanced around. "I mean, I don't want to make you late for your dance preparations."

"No, that's fine. This is important. Paige? Sof? You'll go ahead and explain, mmm?"

They went.

But Lacey—Lacey did not go. Lacey stayed put. And said, "What competition?"

"Oh, you know."

"Because I don't remember you entering an email competition to win a Gucci bag. You say that those competitions are pointless. And you hate designer stuff."

The bracelet was starting to feel like a handcuff or something. I could literally feel my cheeks starting to heat up as I said, "I know! It was a complete mistake, actually. That's what makes it so surprising that I won! Go get your manicure, Lacey," I added. "I don't want to make *you* late too!"

"Where is this bag?" said Savannah.

"I left it in the car. Just around the corner. It won't take a sec."

"Something is going on," said Lacey.

Savannah looked from me to Lacey and back again.

I did my very best to seem completely casual and like I'd accidentally won a horrible-looking Gucci bag. There isn't an obvious face for that. But—

"Okay," said Savannah. "Show me."

"This way," I said, and motioned her around the corner, where Adrian was sitting in the car with the engine running and the back door open. Lacey followed us and stopped at the front door, opening it and peering inside.

Savannah said, "It's in here, right?"

"In the back, that's right," I said, getting behind her as she leaned in, and then, with just one tiny push on her perfect backside, she fell forward, and Jaz rose up from the floorboard and pulled her down, and I hurled in behind her and slammed the door, and Adrian revved the engine, and then we were off, zooming down the main road, and we'd done it, sort of. We'd…

"*Kidnapped me!*" gasped Savannah.

Just as Lacey turned around from the front seat and said, "Katie, what are you *doing?*"

♪ ♫ ♪

It took quite a long time to explain, partly because Savannah kept screaming.

"So, basically, I need to get backstage at the Teen Time Awards."

"Eeeeeeeeeew! This seat fabric is so *icky*!"

"Because I have to apologize to Kurt, and this is the last chance I'll ever get."

"What is *on* this seat belt?"

"And I know everything is ruined, and my life is over, but I thought, if I could make this one thing right…"

"Jaz is looking at me. Make her stop looking."

"Jaz, stop looking at Savannah."

"You know this really *is* kidnapping," said Lacey. "I could call the police."

I saw Adrian's hands stiffen on the steering wheel. "Well, you're not kidnapped, Lace. You chose to get in. But, I guess, yeah. If you wanted to, you could."

And Savannah said, "Where is the bag, please?"

Lacey's groan filled the car. "There isn't a bag, Savannah. It was a way to get you in here. They're using you. To force their way into Karamel's dressing room. They're exploiting your relationship with Kolin."

"But I don't even have a relationship with Kolin," said Savannah.

"What?"

The car began to slow. Along with my pulse.

"You said…" My voice cracked. "You kept talking about how Kolin was your boyfriend."

Savannah was silent.

"Sav?" Lacey leaned around the seat, looking as shocked as I've ever seen her. "Are you all right?"

"Fine, thanks, Lacey," said Savannah, and, OMG, the girl was on the verge of crying.

"Do you want some water?" I said, scrabbling in my bag. "Or, here—I've got a Mars Milk."

She looked like she was going to throw it back in my face, only then, miracle of miracles, she opened it and took a sip. And did this kind of ecstatic groan.

"What is this?"

"It's a Mars Milk."

"I've never…it tastes like…"

"Calories. That's what calories taste like."

She took a long swig and then another. And another. "Er, Sav. You and Kolin…?" Savannah blinked, her eyes deep blue beneath twin pools of tears. "He did text me. He texted me a lot. We texted forever. Only…"

"What?" said Lacey, and she gave Savannah this sweet, kind smile, and I thought, *Sav has a heart. How did I miss this?*

"Only then he said he wanted to meet up. And so I stopped texting him back."

"Why the…?" I started. Then, after Lacey shot me a glare, I added, "Um, I mean, I'm sure you had a very good reason, but…why?!"

Another long swig. "Because...I'm not you, Katie."

"No. You're way better than me."

"I'm way better *looking* than you," corrected Savannah. "But I'm not...I don't have any...talent. I'm just a pretty girl. Like everyone else. Well, prettier than everyone else. But that's it." She sniffed. "Kolin would have found out, and...you may be facially challenged, Katie, but at least you're...original."

Savannah was insecure? Savannah was jealous of *me*?

Genuinely, I don't know anything about anything. "Savannah," I said, "you are completely original. I've never met anyone like you. You're beautiful—"

"I know," said Savannah.

"I mean, inside. You're really funny. Often without realizing it, but hey. Plus, you've been a great friend to Lacey recently. Which is more than can be said for me."

Lacey shifted in her seat.

"In fact," I went on, "I'd say, as far as friends go, I'm pretty much the worst there is."

There was a long pause.

My eyes met Lacey's in the mirror.

"But I can't," said Savannah. "I never texted him back. I can't just suddenly get in contact now. What will he think of me? Don't ask me anymore, Katie. I won't do it. And nothing you can say will change my mind."

Then Adrian said, "If you get us into Karamel's dressing room, Savannah, I'll buy you a Gucci bag."

"Total yes," said Savannah.

That conversation happened during the first part of the car trip, but in fact it was another forty-five minutes before we got to Wembley. Forty-five minutes is really a long time even in a normal situation. Forty-five minutes in a car with a silent ex-best friend, a scary person, and a Savannah is actual forever.

Lacey had her head down and wasn't saying much, which was like having a black hole sitting in the front seat, sucking up every scrap of small talk any of the rest of us managed to generate and making it disappear.

Savannah was scrolling through Gucci bags on her phone.

"Maybe a tote? But, hmm, a waste to get canvas. It won't wear well. I think it has to be leather, yes? Ooh, this one's nice. It's cross-body, and the G's are embossed."

"How much?" said Adrian.

"Eight hundred and fifty."

The car swerved, and we almost went into the median strip.

"You had to say a Gucci bag, didn't you, Katie?" said Adrian. "It couldn't just be Topshop."

"Topshop is okay," said Savannah.

"Great! In that case—"

"For other girls."

"Right."

"In fact, could we consider upgrading to Prada?"

"No."

"Look," I said. "We don't have to do this. It's not like it's the answer to all of my problems. It's not even the answer to some of my problems." I thought and sighed. "It's the answer to one of my problems. One of many. And that's if he even…"

Then, on the horizon, I saw it. That arch. Wembley.

"So here's what we need to do. All very simple. Nothing to get in a panic about," said Adrian, looking rather gray. "We have to get through security and go backstage. And we can't let anyone see Katie. And I don't want to get the car towed, so some kind of permit might be nice."

We all looked at Savannah, who said, "GG Supreme mini chain bag. In a blossom finish. Six hundred is a bargain really."

Swallowing very hard, Adrian nodded, and Savannah lifted her phone to her ear. "Kolin! It's Sav. From the party. I know. I did mean to call…Were you? Were you? Oh, Kolin. You are very sweet."

This went on for a very long time. "Aw."

And on. "Squee!" And on.

Finally, about a year later, I tapped on my watch.

Which Savannah looked at and wrinkled her nose.

"Ew. No, not you! I just saw the most revolting watch."

"Savannah!"

"So here's the thing. I'm actually outside Wembley right now...complete coincidence...yes...oh I know...of course, babes..."

It wasn't working. He was clearly telling her to go away. Because, now that I thought about it, obviously you don't meet up with people you ran into once at a party just before you sing at Wembley Arena. I mean, if you're me, you're too busy puking to even think of using your mouth for anything else.

Only then...

"Yay! So we're in this completely ugly, like, truck thing. It's blue. I know. It does go with my eyes. Thank you. Will you tell the security people? See you in five. Kiss kiss."

"Thank you, Savannah," said Adrian. "Now, Katie, it's up to you."

Chapter Thirty

I'M NOT GOING TO GO into the Savannah/Kolin reunion, which involved the two of them gluing their faces together with Savannah's Crème de la Mer lip balm, while me, Lacey, Jaz, and Adrian stood and admired the wall.

Eventually, after about a hundred thousand years of whispers and giggles, Savannah pointed and said, "Dressing room seven. He's alone. Kristian went to find something to eat." And then she went back to kissing Kolin.

Adrian turned to Jaz and Lacey.

"Should we…go and find a snack?"

"Okay," said Lacey.

"No way. I want to see this. I mean, yeah, all right," said Jaz.

I took a deep breath. And wondered what the point of taking a deep breath was since it never seemed to help.

Then I knocked and went inside.

I guess I'd been expecting Karamel's dressing room to be this kind of luxe palace of gorgeousness with, I don't know, gold walls and a Jacuzzi. Instead, it was just really nice, in that there was a big mirror and a bulletin board and a small table with a huge bunch of white lilies in the middle, which smelled lovely, almost lovely enough to counteract the very strong odor of feet.

Kurt was tuning his guitar when I went in, and he looked up with this great big smile, which, as he saw me, fell off his face and smashed into pieces all over the floor.

"Hi!" I said.

"You?"

He didn't look especially overjoyed that I was there.

In fact, I'd go as far as to say that I was the person he least wanted to see in the entire universe.

"Yes, me."

"Get out."

"Um…"

"Go!"

I didn't—couldn't—move, and that just made him shout louder.

"I supported you from the beginning. Right back when you did your first single and stupid Tony wouldn't release it, I defended you. And I let you put out a song where you basically accused my music, my *art*, of being worthless."

I crumpled as the words hit me.

"I was nice to you. I respected you, even after you dragged me into the stupid Karamel versus Katie fight, which I never wanted because I liked your music. I liked you. And you still thought I'd sell you out to *Pop Trash*, and not only that, you went public and told everyone?! What does that make me look like?" He spun in a small, angry circle. "And why are you still here?"

"Because…I came to take it all back. Okay? I'm a complete idiot, and you don't have to forgive me."

"I wasn't planning to."

Once again, I was realizing the importance of making a plan before you get into the room with someone important.

Only, really, what else could I say? Other than:

"I'm sorry. I'm sorry for all of it. For the song, the stupid, pathetic excuse for a song, which I only wrote to get back at my best friend for ignoring me on my birthday."

He didn't look any happier. He certainly didn't look like the apology was helping. But he didn't throw me out. So:

"And the chart battle, which was low. And pointless. Who cares if some people like one thing and some people like something else? There's room in the world for all of us.

More than that, though, I should never have let it continue, after the concert, when I realized you were good."

"No. You shouldn't have."

I managed to look up and meet his eyes, his huge, beautiful eyes the color of new chestnuts, and saw that he hated me so much.

"I did everything wrong."

"You did."

"And it turns out it was my dad who sold the story about me, if you can imagine how that feels, and Adrian committed to spending a fortune on Savannah to get me in here, so you don't have to listen to my apology, but I do at least have to stand in front of you and say it."

"What the…?"

"I know! But I promised her a Gucci bag. I maybe should have checked the price first, but there we go."

"I meant, the story came from your *dad*?"

"Um. Yeah." I'd promised myself I wouldn't cry, and I almost kept it.

"That's awful."

"He didn't know what he was doing," I said quickly. Then I added, "Which, really, is just as bad as if he did."

"I narrowed it down to either being a teacher or someone your mom works with. Or a friend. Well, a so-called friend."

"He's a so-called dad," I said. "I should've known. I've been so stupid."

I caught a glimpse of myself in that big mirror and looked away. I'm sure that mirror has seen lots of interesting things, being situated in the main dressing room at Wembley Arena. Still, I bet it has never seen anyone produce such a spectacular quantity of snot as me.

Neither, by his expression, had Kurt. Even so, he came and sat next to me, and I saw that something in what I'd said had pierced him somehow. "It's not stupid to love someone. It's not stupid to trust your father."

"No?"

"It's not stupid to have faith in people. Even if they let you down. You keep having faith in them. Maybe they'll live up to it." He smiled that amazing smile. "That's what I tell myself about my dad. It hasn't worked so far. But you never know."

I looked at my feet. "I don't think I have much faith in me anymore."

"Um, quick question—because I do want to talk about this, but we're supposed to be onstage pretty soon—where is Kolin?"

"Oh. Yes. Um, Kolin's with Savannah. They're getting back together." I thought about exactly what this might entail. "You might want to text him."

He did, and I watched his face frowning over his phone.

Not in a weird, stalkery way or anything.

Okay, in a slightly stalkery way. But I don't think it counts as stalking if the person finishes texting and looks up at you and grins.

Which made me blush so much that I looked away and made myself stare very hard at a piece of paper stuck to the bulletin board.

The order of appearances. Which went like this:

TEEN TIME AWARDS

Olly Murs
Ed Sheeran
~~Tinie Tempah~~
Little Mix
Bruno Mars
~~Katie Cox~~
Rita Ora
Karamel

"What's my name doing up there?"

"I thought you won something," said Kurt.

"I did. But they took it away."

"That can't happen."

"No. Except maybe…" My mind rewound to that conversation with Tony on an afternoon where everything had still seemed possible. "I did win something. But that was before…everything…"

"You could still sing, you know," said Kurt in this light voice that completely went against the enormous weight of what he was suggesting.

"Um, ha ha—I don't think so."

"Why not?"

"You want reasons? Okay. For one thing, literally the entire stadium wants me to be erased from the face of the earth. So there's that. Also, I don't have my guitar with me. Also, I'm done with music."

"Katie, you can't give up music."

"Watch me." Not that there was anything to actually watch, but you know.

"You're never going to play again?"

"I made some rules, if you must know. I can't play or sing anything unless I hum something without realizing it, and I'm allowed to sing if it would be weird not to, like, for instance, if I'm at a party and someone brings in a birthday cake. And—"

"You're happy with this? As a decision? For the rest of your life?"

And I wanted to scream at him. That, no, of course I

wasn't happy with it. That I was basically trapping myself in a gray, soulless universe of nothingness, as though all the flavor had been drained from everything that mattered, like when you eat a strawberry in February, only multiplied by everything, for always and ever.

"I just…don't want to make things any worse."

"I guess." He nodded. "Yeah. It's sad, but…it makes sense."

"Yeah."

So that was it then. I'd made my apology.

Everything was finished. I should go home.

Maybe start looking for a Gucci flash sale or something.

Then a voice made me look up. A sweet, tender voice.

Singing a familiar tune.

> Quite like guitar girl
> And I do have a tattoo

Kurt was strumming on his guitar.

> Quite like guitar girl
> Thinking she should get one, too

Then he stopped. "Mine's not Chinese, FYI." He rolled up a sleeve to reveal golden skin and something complicated going on just above his elbow. "It's Celtic. I had it done on tour. In Latvia of all places."

"Cool."

"Not really. My mom went berserk. Technically, I think I'm still grounded."

I found myself smiling. Just a little. "Okay, I'll update it." I lifted the guitar across and into my arms.

> The tattooed Celtic symbol
> On skin that's nicely tanned

"Better?"

"Better," said Kurt. "Anything else you want to change?"

We were very close as I sang.

> Quite like the boy band
> Their upbeat melodies
> Quite like the boy band
> Kinda pop-py kinda cheese
>
> It's cool they love their grannies
> And their devoted fans
> I quite like the boy band

"Only *quite*?" said Kurt.

"More than quite," I said, looking away.

I like the boy band
It's a different way to be
I like the boy band
Their vibe is so happy

And if there's a chance they'll take it
Then I'll offer them my hand
Yes, I like the boy band

I finished, and he took my hand from the strings and held it in his.

It was an amazing moment. Which I ruined, by blurting out, "Look. I said my thing. I should let you get going. With singing to all of Wembley."

"Ed just came off stage. We still have time," said Kurt. Then, seeing my confusion, he added, "Ed Sheeran. He's really nice."

"Oh good," I said. "I'd hate it if he wasn't."

We both looked at the wall and at my name crossed out.

And…it's hard to explain how I could feel so sure of it, but I knew, I just knew, that we had both had the same thought.

"You should—"

"I can't—"

It was so big and so terrible that I couldn't even begin to put it into words.

"Kurt, I *can't*."

"Katie, you can."

"But…I'm giving up music." He didn't say anything. "Everyone hates me."

He still didn't say anything. The messages from Tony's computer screen scrolled invisibly between us. So much hate. Out there. So close. And all of it for me.

"Kurt, it's not… I can't."

His eyes were so gentle, this luscious, delicious brown. Like chocolate mousse. Only then, they frosted over. Like chocolate mousse that's been stuck right at the back of the fridge.

"All right. I thought you were truly sorry. But…"

"I am!"

"Then show me."

"You want me to sing."

"I do."

"You want me to sing 'Can't Stand the Boy Band'? To all of Wembley?"

"I do. I'll even lend you my guitar."

"Wow. Wait. No. Maybe. I mean, I could sing 'Cake Boyfriend.' Or 'Spaghetti Hoops'—no, not that—but I could definitely do 'Leftover Chinese Takeout Blues.' It has a real swing to it…"

Even as I said it, I knew. If I was going to get up there, I had to sing "Can't Stand the Boy Band." Anything else would be a gigantic cop-out.

"I can't do it."

Which is when Jaz came bursting through the door and went: "Ha ha ha, you're Kurt from Karamel, ha ha ha."

"Jaz!"

She was followed by Savannah and Kolin, whose face was covered in Savanna's lip gloss, and Kristian, Adrian, and Lacey, who twiddled her hair and said, "Hi, I love your music. Sorry, just ignore me."

"Please," said Jaz, as my BF stared at the floor. "Hold it together."

"This is Kurt from Karamel!" wailed Lacey.

"And you're Lacey from Harltree." She looked up, and I was just thinking that maybe this was the moment when they might actually become friends, when Jaz followed it up with, "Lacey Daniels, you are slightly less pathetic than you think you are."

Lace made a face.

Jaz made a face. Kurt was laughing.

And I thought, *This is okay actually*. Just, everyone

together, they don't have to be besties or anything. They can mock each other, if they have to. Just…

Oh. My. God. *Oh my God.*

"I know how to do this," I said. "I'm going to do it. I'm going to sing."

"There we go," said Kurt.

"Why?" said Kolin, who was still looking at Savannah.

"You are going to get shredded to pieces," said Lacey.

Chapter Thirty-One

SO THERE I WAS, STANDING in the wings, ready to do my first major concert. I mean, seriously major, with tons of people watching and goodness knows how many more online.

Even though I'd practiced, I was shaking so badly I could barely hold the guitar. My hands were dripping sweat, and there was a good chance that when I opened my mouth, I'd barf all over the stage.

It was no use telling myself that everyone gets nervous. Because this was no ordinary concert.

I was about to sing live to twelve and a half thousand people.

And each and every one of them wanted to kill me.

In fact, it's less complicated than you'd think, getting on the lineup of the Teen Time Awards at Wembley Arena. I mean, it helps if you were on it originally before you got yourself taken off by being dropped from your record label.

Plus, it's an advantage if you have the lead singer of a monstrously famous boy band to talk to the high-up people and convince them that it's a good idea. Backed by your amazing manager, Adrian.

Also, Bruno Mars was stuck in America because his flight had been canceled, and the show was going to be way too short.

So, in the space of approximately ten minutes, I went from being a slightly carsick nobody, wearing my sloppiest sweatpants, with my hair completely everywhere and a breakout so bad that I looked like I was having some kind of allergic reaction to…entirely the same person, only holding Kurt's guitar.

"She cannot go onstage like that," Savannah was saying. "It's like, if you're going to die, you should at least be a beautiful corpse."

"Thanks, Savannah, that's really helpful."

"I…I have some concealer. It's not much. And it's the wrong shade. But…"

The words came from a very unexpected source. "Lace…are you sure?"

"You know you can catch pimples from sharing makeup, don't you?" said Savannah.

"I know," said Lacey.

"You don't have to," I said.

She leaned in to dot and then smear concealer onto my forehead, and I got a close-up of the inside of her mouth as she said, "What you said. In the car. You were a bad friend to me. But I wasn't there for you. On your birthday. And… you're going to get torn apart out there. If this is the last time I see you, I'd rather we said good-bye as friends."

"So…" I didn't know what to say. "Am I allowed to wear my charm bracelet then?"

"If you like," said Lacey.

"I do like," I said, and maybe we would have hugged or maybe we wouldn't have since she still looked a little wary. I have no way of knowing because, just then, a man with a clipboard knocked in that brisk way that means someone's going to come in whether you're sharing an emotional moment or not. And then he came in.

"Katie Cox? Tech team. So it's just you, a mic, and an acoustic guitar?"

"Yeah," I said.

"Nothing for us to project behind you? Everyone else has a video or lights or something."

"No," I said. "Sorry."

"Hey, can I have your phone?" said Jaz.

"Why?"

"Can't tell you now," said Jaz. "But trust me, okay?"

Just to recap. The first time Jaz had held a phone in my presence, she'd put me on the Internet and simultaneously made and destroyed my entire life. The next time I lent her my phone, she'd nearly given my mother a heart attack. So you can see why I wasn't happy about this.

Which I guess is why she just leaned over and grabbed it out of my hand.

"Jaz! Jaz, come back. *Jaz!*"

Clipboard man tapped his clipboard. "If you'd like to follow me upstairs, Katie? You're next."

♪ ♫ ♩ ♬

Up we went. Up and around and along the bright hallways, in this kind of procession of doom, and then suddenly, we could hear them, the crowd, just ahead. Not the noise I'd heard back at my little concert. Not even the shrieking at the Karamel gig.

This was like…the sea. A real sea, an ocean, a swell of sound that went back and back.

"Catch her. She's going down."

"No, no, I'm okay. It's all right," I said. "It's not even that many people really. Is it?"

We'd reached the wings, and I looked out.

And it was huge. Epic. A city of people, of twinkling

phones and glow sticks, neatly stacked in rows that went on and on and on and up and up.

"Good luck, Katie."

"Good luck."

"Good luck."

"RIP, babes." That one was Savannah.

"Now, the original winner of the People's Act Teen Time Award. Kind of a controversial one… This award was decided before recent…events , and was later changed. But she's here now with her new song. It's *Katie Cox*!"

I don't know if you've ever heard twelve and a half thousand people gasp all at the same time.

It's truly something. Then silence.

My legs were carrying me out into the light. Down onto the little stool they'd put there.

Fingers, shaking, into place on the guitar, as the first boos began.

A chord.

The wrong chord. Stop.

Take a breath.

More boos. Louder now. Then…

Quite like the boy band

A wave of jeering.

Their upbeat melodies

Keep going, Katie.

Quite like the boy band
Kinda pop-py kinda cheese

It's cool they love their grannies
And their devoted fans

I quite like the boy band

And then—they cheered!
Not loudly. And not for long. But they did.

I like the boy band
It's a different way to be
I like the boy band
Their vibe is so happy

Another cheer. Big enough to drown out the boos, which were still coming. I felt my voice lift, as though I'd stepped from a boat onto solid ground.

And if there's a chance they'll take it

Then I'll offer them my hand
Yes, I like the boy band

Something was happening. The glowing phones, which had been waving in all different directions...they were all waving...together.

I went into the instrumental section, which was very tricky, and so maybe that's why the crowd noticed before I did...and it was only when I heard this infinite screaming roar that I realized...

Kurt was next to me. And he sang:

Quite like guitar girl
And I do have a tattoo
Quite like guitar girl
Thinking she should get one, too

Her lyrics make me chuckle
But her bedroom makes me hurl
Yeah, I quite like guitar girl

And something made me glance back up, behind us...

I don't know how Jaz did it.

But there was my face, singing in my bedroom. Then Karamel, sitting in their camper van. Then, the messages, from me to Kurt, from Kurt back to me. And the comments, all of them, the love and the hate, flashing faster and faster and faster…

And we sang:

> Let's make a new band
> While the music's feeling right
> Let's start a new band
> Singing out into the night
>
> Yes if there's a chance you'll take it
> Then I'm giving you my hand
> You and me, a new band

Kurt was clapping, and I held out the mic, like I'd only ever seen on TV, the charms on my bracelet flashing under spotlights hotter than the sun.

"Sing with me, Wembley."

> Yes if there's a chance you'll take it
> Then I'm giving you my hand
> Just tonight, a new band

They sang in a way I couldn't just hear but feel. They sang it over and over and over again.

In the wings, Savannah and Adrian were singing. And Lacey was singing.

And even, wow—even Jaz.

When Vernon Kay came bounding onto the stage and said, "Give it up for Katie Cox!" I kind of hardly noticed.

The applause began, and I lifted my arms.

"Peace and love," said Kurt. "Peace and love."

A microphone was shoved into my face. "Katie?"

"Peace and love," I said.

And then I cracked up, because, I mean, *honestly*.

Chapter Thirty-Two

AFTERWARD, EVERYTHING WENT BERSERK.

My plan had been to hide in the dressing room or maybe get back into the car and go home, but instead we got swept along by the clipboard people into this gigantic room, which pulsed and throbbed with lights and music and was completely packed with people wearing special wristbands and very little else, all drinking champagne like they were dying of thirst or something.

"Bruno's going crazy that he missed it. Heads will roll."

And: "They didn't do that at the sound check."

And: "Are those two an item? There's definitely something going on there."

I kind of shuffled in, still horribly aware that I had my sweats on and only the very minimum of makeup, and stood in the corner trying not to look at anyone.

Which was really difficult, as everyone—and I mean *everyone*—wanted to look at me.

I had pretty much the whole of the iTunes Top 100 come up and congratulate me, which was nice although deeply embarrassing, and once Jaz had given me my phone back, I got some cool selfies, which was even nicer, but nicest of all was the green-apple-flavored Perrier that Lace brought over. In the end, Lacey, Jaz, and Adrian had to form a protective circle so I could drink it.

Which was an okay way of spending the party, pointing and laughing at the various insane outfits everyone had turned up in, until Adrian stepped back to say, "Katie. It's Tony."

At the exact same time, my phone started ringing. "Sorry," I said. "Important phone call… Oh…" It was Dad. I hit Reject, then looked up to do the same to my ex-label boss.

He was right in front of me, his teeth glowing in the ultraviolet light. Or maybe there wasn't any ultraviolet. Maybe they were just glowing anyway. Maybe they weren't even teeth, just two rows of tooth-shaped light bulbs.

"Look—" I began, not really knowing where I was going with this, but feeling like I needed to say something.

"I know."

"It's just…" I hid my face in my glass.

"I'll say it, okay? We shouldn't have dropped you so fast."

"I understand why you did." Which was true. "I would have done the same if I were you."

"Be that as it may, I was actually coming over to

suggest you join another label. There's a job for your dad whatever you do, of course, but we're assuming you'll want to go elsewhere."

What?

"Oh. Right." My brain finally caught up with the conversation. "And actually, you were the one who set up the whole Karamel-rivalry-single-release-on-the-same-day thing. So you shouldn't have dropped me so fast!"

"No," he said.

"I should join another label?!"

"You should. We're too easily scared by bad press. We'd never had a situation like that, and we panicked. It was irresponsible, and it was unkind. It won't happen again, but of course, you'll want to go elsewhere. I'm thinking Monumental Beats would be a good place for you. I'll get you a meeting with Scarlett. Or there's FRD. Bethany's a peach…"

"I don't need another label," I said. "I'm not doing music anymore. I'm going back to being normal."

"Katie." He stood next to me, and we looked out over the room. The woman closest to us was wearing a top open almost to the waist. She lifted her arm to wave and flashed me. "You can't go back to normal, Katie. You've gone too far for that."

"I haven't. It's only been a few weeks, but it'll happen." I tried not to think about that hideous night at the Harvester. "It might be a while, but I will."

"Your song. Just now. It's the number one trending topic worldwide."

"Look, Tony, no one says 'trending topic,' just like no one says 'social media' and…" I digested what he'd just told me. "Come again?"

"Your performance just now is the number one trending topic on the planet."

"I don't…"

"People are saying you've brought whole worlds of music together. You've become this symbol of reconciliation. Of friendship."

"In the last half hour?!"

"Doesn't take long."

"They'll forget. Everyone will forget."

"If that's what you want."

Then Jessie J came over. In real life, her hair looks even better than it does on TV, super glossy and perfectly straight.

Eventually she went off to talk to Emeli Sandé, and Tony turned back to me with a sad smile.

"Is there anything I can say? You're a marvel, Katie. You have the world at your feet. That, there, tonight—*that's* your single. The live recording. I've already had calls from about nine different countries. We'll put it on the album with 'Just Me,' 'Cake Boyfriend,' 'Autocorrect'—maybe not the one about spaghetti hoops…but otherwise, you can choose. We won't interfere. And then…your summer vacation is coming up, isn't it? How would you like to come with us to the States? The UK—that's great, that's all well and good, but we need to be thinking globally now. We'll fly you first class. You can bring a friend, if you want. Two friends. We'll put you up somewhere fancy. Get you the best of everything. All you need to do is sing like you did tonight."

"I can't. I made the decision. That was my last song."

He sighed. "Look. Katie. I know I'm the villain. But just tell me this. Has anyone, *anyone*, heard your plan to give up music and told you that it's a good idea?"

I didn't want to have to shake my head. And, as it turned out, I didn't have to.

"You know where to find me," said Tony. "Whether you want to stay with Top Music, sign with a new label, whatever. Like it or not, you're a star now."

I spent a few minutes gazing out into that crowded room and thinking how incredibly upsetting it was that I didn't feel like I fit in here anymore than I did at school, and really, wasn't there a single party in the world where a girl could have a good time?!

Then I took my phone onto the balcony to tell the one person who definitely would approve of my decision.

"Hi, Mom."

"Katie. I am going to kill you. Honestly. The second I get my hands on you…I am going to…I'm…so…I'm so…"

"Mom, are you *crying*?"

"I'm so proud of you."

"Oh. Okay."

"The last few days have been appalling. Then I get a message from Ade. We put the TV on, me and your father. One minute, we're seeing *Coronation Street*, the next, we're watching our little girl lighting up London."

"Well…"

"And I don't like it. I don't."

"I know."

"But I see now, you've got to do this, don't you?"

Now I was crying a little. "I don't know if I can. What you said, about not getting hurt. I'm going to get hurt, aren't I?"

"Yes. But…you'll get hurt anyway. Whatever you do. I can't protect you forever."

"I don't think I'm strong enough."

"I know you are, Katie."

"Mom—" I let the pause sit between us for a while because it seemed to say what I wanted to better than words. Then I said, "Mom, it was Dad. He was the one who sold the story."

"He told me."

"I'll never forgive him."

A snort. "It's not the worst thing he's ever done."

"I kn-know. He's been…he shouldn't have… Ending it with you and then running off to America with Catriona and blowing all that money and then… I get it now. And I'm never going to speak to him again. I promise you that."

"Katie, your father is a total idiot. A complete and utter—" She stopped herself. "But of course you'll speak to him again. He's your dad. He loves you. And…it's hard for him, being the brilliant, talented idiot that he is and having to live with himself."

"So?"

"So…when you were onstage tonight, I saw him. In you."

"No!"

"He's a part of you," said Mom. "He knows he did the wrong thing. He understands that."

Since when did Mom stand up for Dad?

"He's here. Next to me. He wants to say sorry. I do think he means it. Will you speak to him, Katie?"

"Not now," I said. "Maybe later." I wiped my eyes. "Is Mands around?"

"Hold on. She just walked through the door. *Amanda, your sister wants to talk to you.*"

"How was the gig? Was the shop full? Did people come?" I was babbling.

"What about *you*?! I just read about everything on my

phone. You are nuts, you know that? Totally nuts… Katie? Katie, what's wrong?"

"Dad," I said. "I've just…Mom said…" I tried to pull myself together. "I can't forgive him. Can I? I don't think I can."

"I'm trying," said Mands.

"He'll go back to America soon," I said. "He has a job waiting for him."

"Maybe you'll find it easier that way," said Amanda, so gently that it made my eyelids prickle.

Which I wanted to believe. I really did.

He's so proud of you, Catriona had said. *He loves you so much.*

Then I knew.

That if I let him go, I'd be letting go of a part of myself. Someone who, yes, was totally and completely selfish. Then again, I hadn't been much better lately.

And to forgive people, to love people, you have to be there.

Oh, Dad.

As I made the decision, then and there, Lacey appeared on one side of me and Jaz on the other.

"Lacey was worrying about you," said Jaz. "I said she's probably doing shots with someone from the show."

"Which would be very worrying," said Lacey. She

peered at me. "*Have* you been doing shots? You look awful. Talk to me, Katie. Talk to me!"

What I wanted to say was that I'd never really meant to bring the world back together.

But then, I hadn't especially meant to tear it apart. "Ugh! That is revolting."

We looked down to see Savannah and Kolin kissing underneath a whole bunch of twinkle lights. Savannah was holding Kolin's head between her hands, presumably to prevent any chance of him escaping.

"So is Kurt going to be your boyfriend?" said Lacey.

"Er, no. I am not the sort of person who goes out with someone in a boy band, thank you very much."

"Aren't you? Because when you two were onstage…it looked like…you might…"

"No way!" I caught myself. "Well, I dunno. He'd have to ditch the fake tan and all those hairstyles. But he's a decent enough guitarist."

"Not to mention incredibly good-looking and an amazing singer and, um, the most desirable boy on the planet."

"Yeah," I said, turning very, very red. "Even so, though, I'm not exactly going to take him to the school dance, am I?"

"Probably not," said Lacey. "Given that it was tonight. I guess if we got in the car right now…we'd catch the part where everyone leaves and goes home."

"What?" This was not good. "You missed it? For this? Lacey, I owe you. Big time."

"S'okay. Wouldn't have been much fun without you, anyway."

"You're a good friend, Lacey Daniels."

"And you, Katie Cox, are a lousy one. It's lucky you can get me into such cool parties."

"The best friend ever," I said.

"Ahem."

"And so are you, Jasmine James. Although I don't remember giving you permission to go broadcasting the contents of my phone to all of Wembley Arena."

"Like I need your permission," murmured Jaz.

We stood there, the three of us, and watched the party. "So…are you doing anything good this summer?"

"Mom was talking about us going to Tenerife, but she hasn't booked it yet because she says the best deals are always last minute. But she said that last year, and then she couldn't get one, so we ended up in Monmouth."

Jaz said, "Why?"

"I was thinking," I said. "How would you like to come with me to America?"

Lacey began to scream so loudly that I didn't hear Jaz's reply.

And she continued screaming, and maybe I did too,

down the stairs and back into the car, with Adrian and (a reluctant) Savannah, all the way back to Harltree.

The lights whizzed past on the highway, Beyoncé came through loud on the stereo, and Adrian rolled down the windows so that the warm night could flow over us.

Lacey was teaching Jaz this special dance you can do sitting down, Beyoncé was Beyoncé, her voice flying like rockets, while Savannah was compiling a complicated order of beauty products that apparently you can only get in the United States.

And while all this was happening, a part of me was thinking about Dad, and whether he'd have time to hang out between doing whatever work Tony was finding for him. Another part of me was googling my name, and then having to stop because it seemed like the rest of the Internet had been pretty much put on hold to make way for stuff about Katie Cox.

Most of me, though, was laughing and singing and doing fancy footwork in the back of that car.

I didn't know whether I was making the right decision. Maybe no one ever does.

But I wasn't saying good-bye to music. Not now, not anytime soon.

Whatever it meant, wherever it led. And that, at least, felt right.

ABOUT THE AUTHOR

Marianne Levy spent her twenties as an actor. She was in various TV shows and made a brief appearance in the film *Ali G Indahouse*, where she managed to forget both her lines. She's been the voice of a leading brand of makeup, a shopping center, and a yogurt company. Marianne is a regular contributor to the *Independent* on Sunday. She lives in London with her husband, daughter, and a bad-tempered cat. Learn more at mariannelevy.com.